MEXICAN PHANTSY

MEXICAN PHANTSY

Short Stories
By
Lauren Napa

Dedication

This book is dedicated to my mother who instilled in me the appreciation of literature and the arts.

To my ancestral home of Deva, Spain whose blood gives me strength.

Preface

I was told I had fire in my eyes when I was born.

Therefore, I write

Contents

The Ides of October

Silent Gladiator

A Mestizo Autumn

House of Cages

About the Author

THE IDES OF OCTOBER

DARE TO DEFY THE ARCANUM ARCANORUM...

LAUREN NAPA

Lips of a Sinner

On an evening when the moon was in Pisces, Father Ignatius Traebello hollered obscenities at Saraphina Cazares y Silvana and threw her out of the confessional.

"Crazy bibber!" she yelled, fleeing St. Ann of the Divine Innocents to the utter bewilderment of the parishioners. Humiliated, she ran behind the time-worn rectory and into the cemetery where the first priests rested in peace. Falling to her knees, she let out uncontrolled moans. After composing herself, she leaned against a tilted gravestone, uprooted from gnarled crabgrass, and recited five Our Fathers and nine Hail Mary's. Then made the Sign of the Cross. That was good enough to forgive herself.

There was no doubt in the holy eyes and ears of Father Traebello. He had seen and heard it. A wicked germ peering at him through the latticed opening. Evil knew what it was doing. Those possessed scarlet lips that spoke to spirits, lips of a sinner murmuring breathlessly, intimating the unspeakable, trying to seduce his mind with the history of corporeality between man and spirits. No. There would be no absolution for the penitent. He would tell the Monsignor in the morning, and they would record the violation against the church and send the documents to Rome. He reached for the fifth of Rye beneath his seat, finished it off and flashed the confessional light for the next penitent.

Shame of Youth

The next morning Muneca Silvana flung open Saraphina's bedroom door. "Get up mensa. You've got some explaining to do before you leave for your flight."

"Aye Mom, I don't know what you're talking about."

"Genevive Toledo called me before her rooster cocked and gave me an earful about your pendejadas in confession."

"Oh, that. Tell that nosey barrel I'm not stupid."

Muneca paused and took off a slipper. She walked to the side of the bed. "Que humillante."

"Mom, not the chancla. The priest likes to tip. I smelled his whiskey blasts through the lattice."

She rolled out of bed.

"Don't talk about Father Traebello like that, "said Muneca pacing back and forth, lamenting about the horror of it all. "It's my week to take dinner to the Rectory. How will I face him?"

"He's sloshed all the time; he won't remember jack. That gringo is old school, I bet he rides a horse to the mini market for his firewater." She snorted. " Leave me alone. Jolie's coming and we must pick up our academic visas."

"Atrevida! You have no filters on your mouth. God's going to punish you if you keep it up." She raised her chin with an air. " I told Genevive your cries were the shame of youth. No thanks to you I had to remind her that the blood of hidalgos flows within us, and we can trace our family name to 1346. We are nobility."

"That again? Oy, nobody cares mom."

"And why you visit Romania and not Spain? Did that bohemian friend of yours talk you into that? Your father would turn over if he knew I let you go to another country unescorted. He always said you were an impetuosa."

"I earned a full scholarship and I intend to honor it. Chill mom, sheesh."

Saraphina finished packing and lifted her crucifix from a jewelry tree. She did a once over. "Don't take liquor to the rectory. I mean it."

A honk attracted their attention. Jolie La Fleur left her Hyundai idling in the driveway and rang the doorbell before Muneca could start again.

"I'll text you when we arrive in Bucharest. Love you." She kissed Muneca's pudgy cheek.

"Aye dios mio," she said blessing her three times. "Hija, no speaking to spirits. I'm warning you. You're just like your father."

"Morning," said Jolie pushing back thick glasses.

"Hey!" Saraphina tossed her luggage into the back seat. "Did you pick up the Romanian maps from the Auto Club?"

"I sure did. Interesting enough, they show backroads leading to preserved medieval towns, castles, old churches and get this, Bran Castle."

"An orgy for our minds. Remember that lecture Professor Castroverde gave on demons and the folklore of old Europe? He spawned my thesis."

"Which demon in particular?"

"The Beast and his influence in arcane mysticism, writings, etcetera. You?"

"The role of Christianity and Martyrs' in ancient Romania," she said turning into the parking lot of the Romanian consulate. "I found where the internet cafés are. We're set. Did you bring the research notes and sea salt?"

"Shoot, I forgot the salt."

"We'd better get some. Romania is loaded with demons."

They laughed.

On their way to the airport, they stopped at the Owl Market, picked up two Blistex, Doritos, an eyeglass repair kit, and a box of sea salt which they would lose on the airport shuttle.

Abracadabra Obscura

On the ides of October, while traveling through an unheard-of village in Romania, Saraphina and Jolie stopped at a curio shop aptly named "Abracadabra Obscura" to escape the snow. A taxidermized owl greeted them silently from a shelf as they shook off the flakes. The darkly furnished shop smelled of old paper, leather, and faint cat urine. There were two over-sized yellow candles dripping wax unto saucers filled to the brim.

While rummaging the back of the shop, Saraphina found a curious book laden with ancient dust. She blew off the silt. The book was the color of dry crushed leaves, its cover revealing what looked like the number two surrounded by tiny, dulled rubies.

"The symbols are evil," said Jolie, stepping back.

"This is exactly what's needed for our research," she replied, fingering her crucifix. "I don't believe you can get any more folkloric than this."

Just then, the keeper stepped in, his bleak smile addressing the customers. He had a complexion of cherry-bark, a thickened jaw, a parrot nose, and was hollow-cheeked. Shabby clothes hung, held up by rawboned shoulders. He lumbered over, one leg shorter, looking annoyed.

A bluster of frigid wind blew in, snapping open the shop's door, sprinkling flurries that prickled their skin.

"I see you found The Vyye," he said edging closer. He didn't bother to shut the door but stared hauntingly as a torrid galaxy swirled within each pupil. After a moment of dead quiet he said, "I will let you have it for cheap. It's lived here way too long and has caused too much trouble for me."

Saraphina's eyes brightened. "Where did it originate?"

"It was brought to Romania by a Roman general who practiced black art rituals in secret. He belonged to the Obscura Malum, a powerful cult. He hid it in a temple that once existed on this property. It was brought to me by descendants of this village before it could be destroyed by religious devotees that roamed this region."

"What kind of black arts? What did he intend?"

"How do I know? I no longer want it here. Do you want it or not?" he hissed, vibrating the thinning purple bags under his eyes.

Victoria startled. She thought she heard a rush of demons' escape the phantom ancient temple.

Against the hard-nosed warning of her schoolmate, Saraphina made the purchase.

"It's late. There's an inn at the corner that's open all night. Make sure you stay there. It's comfortable and safe from marauders. You can leave your car here; I'll keep a watch on it. And don't read the book in the hours of the dark when the moon puts down the red sun," he said practically shoving them out the door. They heard his guffaws over the tinkling of bells while hanging the "Closed" sign, locking the door behind them.

"Are you mad? That guy's a creep. Did you get a load of his eyes?" said Jolie, shuddering. "What's up with that red sun thingy he talked about? "

"Who cares? I can't wait to peruse this. Let's get a room. I'm so hungry, I could eat my shoes.

The Vyye

When the shroud of night entombed the moon, while Jolie slept, Saraphina unbound The Vyye beside the flickering light of a bent sallow candle. "Ven a mi," she whispered and waited.

Mists of violet symbols rose from its pages, whirling and wailing bedevilments. She drew back, tipping the burning candle. The Beast emerged amidst the sorcery, a grotesque face fluttering in the golden light of the candle. Its ghosted hands garroted her neck as it greedily inhaled and stole her last breath before she could scream. After swallowing her soul, he whisked her flesh to the hosts of hell. He flicked his tongue into the air, tasting his triumph, then disappeared into the pall.

Singe

After the red sun defeated the moon, Jolie woke to the odor of acrid sulphur. It reminded her of the smell the mortuary next door to her parent's house puffed on Tuesdays and Thursdays.

On the desk was a scintillating Vyye, flashing sparks of violet. Aside it, lay a burnt hand clutching a singed crucifix.

Jolie, heart hammering, rose to run. But no door existed.

SILENT
GLADIATOR
LAUREN NAPA

Father Christoph

A steady patter of drizzle rushed my face as I hastened out the door of my Mediterranean style condominium I had busted my rear for years to purchase located in one of the better suburbs of Los Angeles.

Today, I chose to wear a little brown dress, san panties of course, thigh-high boots and my fav parfum, Natalie. Shouts of "Don't forget to pick up my smokes and toe fungus medicine" trailed me out the front door. I was so relieved to step away from the loathsome slug and his cigarette funk

I drew a breath and opened my umbrella. Freedom! At least for the day.

A rusty hinge creaked behind me. I turned, shuddered. It was Earle standing on the second step waving his arms, yelping, still wearing the same last few nights' marinara stained tee shirt.

"I forgot. Bring beer, Cheetos, and hot dogs. Oh yah, and Beano!"

I nodded. Under my umbrella I cursed the damned leech. I would walk with my compadre, sin. And nobody could stop me.

It was Thursday, the day of the week I reveled. I loved that walk on the eastside of La Sirena Park where the begonia's little faces smiled at me, and the violets seemed to wish me a saucy day. The rain was letting off and the sun was busying itself shooing away the clouds. My hiney was covered in goosebumps and intimated to my little brown dress that it was rather brisk.

I thought about the plight of the Monarch butterflies nearing extinction, the COVID pandemic and the California wildfires…anything to take my mind off that chronic unemployed gas-passing slug I had married twelve years ago. He stopped attending law school the day after I achieved my position at the University, feigning sciatica attacks, high blood pressure and vertigo. He hadn't seen the likes of any education or work since. "I like to be spoiled," he would tell me. I wish I could give that slug back to his parents.

I had no idea who mine were, or where I came from. I knew I was Latina, that's what the orphanage priest, Father Christoph, my paternal figure told me, who wholeheartedly loved and believed in me. Always the adulator, I cherished his guidance. I loved him so much; I told him everything about my daily doings and even when my first cycle had arrived. He told me stories about how he grew up in a little village in Spain where he raised miniature horses and goats and how he was called to the Roman collar. I even confessed to him that I wanted to marry him when I turned eighteen because he was so beautiful looking and treated me like a princess. He would hug me and laugh. But I never told him that I lusted for him. I knew it was taboo, but I would have him one day.

I was one of those innocent young women whose mantra was "Say yes to the dress" which I blindly followed. My naïve romantic idealism of 'find-my-hero' had cost me financially, mentally, and left me sexually deprived. One would think that an anthropologist with a doctorate would have known better and fled the early stages of an incoming train wreck. But no, not me. Oh no, the sweet short-sighted guilt-riddled Catholic girl. Fuck me to tears.

I dreaded coming home from work, where that oppressive black cloud hovered over my home. I shrugged off the thoughts. Not today. Never mind the slug. I had fallen hard for the Professor. In fact, too hard. He had rekindled my soul.

Eren's Tapas

I strolled down Union street, took a sharp left on Grande Sur, and stopped at Eren's Tapas, famous for its Spanish delicacies. As I entered, savors of Spanish spices and garlicky olives tickled my nose. Eren's shop was warm, always polished, and clean. The delicious aromas of fresh baked bread, tortilla de patatas, and pungent cheeses floated about. Mouth- watering cuts of Jamon Serrano hung from the ceiling. Bottles of Rioja wine sat in sets over a sparkling glass case calling me to entertain them. I tinkled the call bell. Eren, a mature graceful woman emerged with a tray of hot almond galletas wearing a traditional Flamenco peineta, a Spanish comb. Once a Flamenco dancer, she was the widow of a famous matador who had left her big money. I always teased her about finding me one.

"Senora Lucretia, how are you? What antojitos would you like today?" Her emerald eyes twinkled.

"Buenos días Eren! Something incredibly special today - for discriminating tastes. A present for a colleague. A sensuous theme would be good." *Did I just say that? Shit.* A big red tide rush my face. "Er, for a woman."

She arched a brow, her lips curling into a curiously dainty smile. "I've a charming basket that will please the most finicky."

I panned the case and made the choices he would appreciate, two jamon bocadillos, a bottle of sparkling Spanish hard cider, a Rioja and two-mile-high crème acunas for "after."

"Your crucifix, beautiful sapphires. Is that new?"

"It is. A gift from Father Christoph before he passed. It came with a beautiful prayer inside a box he carved for me."

"Awe si. It's exquisite. Pobre padre. You were close to him. I could see in your eyes you took his death hard hija."

"I did. I miss him so much, it hurts."

"It's sad when the sun sets early on the good."

Eren busied herself prepping the gift, humming what sounded like Bolero.

"For your colleague."

"I love it! Exactly what I envisioned. Gracias!"

I floated her a kiss, paid, and tipped her generously.

"Gracias Senora Lucretia."

"You're welcome." I sauntered out without a care in the world and made my way to Hotel Bella Pacifica.

Professor Reginald Chad Worthington

Thursdays. Ah, my precious Thursdays. Secret and mine. I had worked it out with the University that I could do my research from home. It would save them money, I said. No guards to post in the lab, I said. No support staff to maintain, I said. Energy efficient, I said. Their accountants thought it brilliant. A perfect stage, and Earle believed Thursdays would be the days I worked overtime at the University.

The University is where I met Dr. Reginald Chad Worthington, the "Silent Gladiator" as I named him. A quiet, ultra-refined 6'3" Black masterpiece of a man who, in my opinion, had been chiseled by Michelangelo. All he had to do was stand there and you were taken. Soon, he would claim victor over your soul, gutting your heart and loins till they begged for mercy. Whispers and first -hand knowledge proclaimed him a powerful lecturer. Mesmerized, his students watched his tight muscles glide magically across the classroom. He'd been likened to a male Medusa, his infectious smile inducing many a shit-faced - turned- to -stone fool. You had to be blind not to notice the outline of his thick baton, taut against his slacks, down almost to his knee. Professor Worthington evoked provocative sensations as I sat in on his lectures. I had to excuse myself several times to release myself in the restroom. His ancient history classes were the first to fill up and there were always students ready to crash his classes. I had an edge, I'm staff and wouldn't hesitate to exploit my position to attend his lectures.

On the first Wednesday of a foggy April morning, I was required to attend a staff meeting with ten others to discuss social distancing while educating. The outdated conference room was boiling hot, stank of long-ago wood, cheap perfume, and vintage women. I was seated at a scarred oak table with a group of female professors. Some were holding pencils, scribbling down notes of nothing. Others had pens, twirling circles onto lined paper of squiggles which looked like big fat ripe figs. I took out my iPad to take notes. Their topic of discussion was not education. It was Professor Worthington.

The conversations were delightfully heated. "Too bad he's engaged to that mousy Philomena Cornell, comes from a high falootin' WASP family." "Her father is preening him for politics," they said. "She nabbed that prize quick," they said. "He's not married yet. I would do him in a New York minute," followed by, "He's too respectful to stray." "Oh really? Men will be men. How about that enormous bulge?" They laughed.

I coughed, swigged down a huge gulp of frog piss coffee, and choked.

Euniss turned. "What's the matter Lucretia?" she said patting my back.

"Coffee down the wrong pipe." I gasped, blotting my chin.

"You sure?" she jested.

That same day, I did a search in the University's Board and Staff Members information pages. There he was. Reginald Chad Worthington, Ph.D., History., Summa cum laude. His expertise was in the government systems of the ancient world and the mysticism of the concubines of that time. Intriguing. I eyed his habits for a week or so. He was pretty much regimented.

Time for a plan. I changed my walking route, hoping to cast a beguiled net over Professor Worthington. The times we passed in the hall, I made sure he noticed my lips, curling him a wide juicy smile as he strode by. Each time, I moved closer and closer, so close that I detected his Chanel cologne drifting over his squeaky-clean body. Be still, heart. On some days, I oiled my breasts with argan, rubbing them till they took on a satiny blush. I removed all the cotton high-collared blouses from my closet, selecting the low thin silky blouses with the v-cuts to work their magic. It did. He noticed.

"Miss. Miss!"

I swiveled.

"You dropped this." With a genuine spark of concern, he held out the Montblanc I'd dropped on purpose. He walked over.

"Thank you, Professor." I raised my brow. "I'm Lucretia," I purred.

"Staff member. You attend my lectures." He moved in closer I assumed because of students needing to pass. "Interested in ancient history?"

"I am. Intriguing subject. You mentioned traveling to many of those sites that no longer exist. I find you, ah, er, your lectures fascinating." I was gibbering.

He moved closer, towering over me. He leaned in moistening his lips. "Your pen Mademoiselle." His nose brushed my nape. I felt his warm breathe take me in.

"Your scent. Beautiful. Reminds me of a village I visited in France, St. Paul de Vence."

"Thank you, it's called Natalie, after Natalie Wood." I blushed. "I believe the base is gardenia."

"I'm not referring to that scent."

Thursdays in La Sirena Park

Me and Reginald started meeting at Eren's Tapas on Thursdays for morning coffee for weeks on end. Communication was easy with him. We spoke openly about our situations, our partners and our future vision for our careers and lives. When talking wasn't enough, we realized we wanted privacy and took to meeting at La Sirena Park, in a secluded part of a maze where people were too lazy to figure out how to escape its swaggle of thick bushes. It was our dream retreat. At first it was sweet teasing and gentle hugs. Then came touches, singed with heat. Then deep kisses, our tongues like heat- seeking missiles which turned into powerful dry humping and groping.

I was falling hard for this man. My body could no longer be sustained with these futile and impotent attempts at passion.

On one late September Thursday at the park, he pulled me close, rubbing his huge member against my gold-tufted triangle.

"Lucretia, I need to release myself in you. It's torturing me," he sighed.

In a heated frenzy, he tore off my panties, threw them into the bushes and unzipped his slacks. After much jostling, he jockeyed out his rock-hard elephantine shaft.

A breath got caught in my throat. I've never seen one so huge. I was throbbing, rheuming. I was at the mercy of my lust, and knew it was wrong. Who cared if he was engaged?

I tiptoed, frenched him deep, sucking on his generous lower lip while fondling his immense iron. My tongue danced across his chest, teasing it, tasting his every inch. I tilled his nipples with small bites. My tongue performed a ballet following a line to his naval, then down to the black tufts of curly ebony hair till I reached his massive staff. Gawd-damn, my nipples were hard.

My lushy was throbbing. I licked and moistened my lips. I started with wet licks to the underside of the great vein. He moaned. His rod jerked and abruptly curved upward. I moistened him with my rheum. All my pleasure points flamed with lust. I flicked my tongue over the mushroom head, sucking gently, then wildly at the tip. He pleaded for more. I plunged my wet lips down his blue-veined pipe, tightened my mouth grip, and gave him a Latine sump-pump like he's never had. Keeping my lips tight and moist, I fingered up his anus for the ultimate pleasure. He grabbed my hair.

" It's coming." His eyes rolled back.

I pulled away. His throbbing erection pained for release. I went down on him again, tonguing his great vein. He seized a clump of hair from the back of my head. I pulled away again, and his spatter pearled my chest.

"We're going to do this right. Your string- of- pearls will be released in me, not on my chest anymore," I whispered.

Suddenly he bent over, groping himself. "My gawd, I've never had a blow like that." He was sucking air, his breaths coming short.

"I want you for the whole day. You and me."

"Yes, yes…I get it," he breathed, slightly bent over, holding himself." He was hard again.

He stood, hands on his swollen Black power, trying to calm it down.

"See what you do to me? " He cast his eyes to the sky and took in a breath. He then flashed his demi-god smile. "So, next Thursday morning. Nine-ish? You good with that?"

"I'm good."

"Hotel Bella Pacifica. I'll book under the name of Somes. We'll celebrate our first union." He winked, kissed my nape while his hands roamed my breasts. "Sorry about your panties," he breathed.

Hotel Bella Pacifica

On Thursday the sixteenth of October I was up early. Emboldened. I scrubbed, waxed, and oiled my landing strip. Earthquakes couldn't stop me.

It was nine in the morning when I left Eren's Tapas, basket in hand and headed for Hotel Bella Pacifica. And just brisk enough for my nipples to "pop."

The hotel was grand, of the art deco silver screen era. The entire copper roof gleamed majestically with columns of thinly veiled goddesses supporting the structure. Good fortune symbols with Sumerian inscriptions were on either side of the hotel's entry. Marble steps led up to the double doors of the glorious icon which must have cost a fortune to build back in the day.

A hefty no lipped woman was at the front desk reading the Enquirer.

"Good morning. May I help you?" She eyed my clothes, practically leaping over the counter to what I'd venture to say to see if she could make out my crouch.

"I've a booking under Somes."

Her cheap gooey nylon lashes cast me the stink-eye. *Sure, you do, tart.*

She eyed the basket.

"How nice of you to bring a picnic," she said with crusty lips. "Mr. Somes is in room 705, seventh floor. Take the elevator and turn left."

"We cannot be disturbed. We have international conference calls coming in."

"Aren't you cold honey?" She kept up the perpetual smirk.

There was sweet sarcasm in her voice. *Smirky biotch.* I threw her a friendly scowl.

When I key-carded the door, there he was. Ready. Sultry. Half under the sheets, swirling a glass of spell-weaving elixir on ice. His tented erection was as prominent as Cleopatra's needle, and I soon would rush like the Nile to be beside him.

The room boasted an elaborate décor. Overhead, a five-bladed fan whirred soft breezes over a heavily carpeted room. The furnishings were reminiscent of the Golden Age of Hollywood, with intricately carved pieces of domestic animals accenting the arms and legs of each sitting piece. A fireplace burned with dancing flames that flickered in tandem to the sultry blues playing in the background. There was a table with a jungle scene akin to an African jungle-hunt movie of some sort. Braided gold tassels held back heavy crimson- and aurum-colored drapes, displaying two floor length windows that led out to a balcony. Photos of Jean Harlow, Ava Gardner, Marlon Brando, Laurel and Hardy and James Dean told their depictive stories from across the room. A glamorous portrait of Hedy Lamarr, dressed in black velvet with diamond chandelier earrings had been placed over the California King. She had been posed with an atom in her delicate palm to celebrate her discipline. It was a premiere room.

"Come here," he beckoned.

"Right," I said, nervously placing our feast on the entry table. I removed my boots, slid off my dress and snaked my way to him.

As I approached, he threw aside the crisp sheets, exposing himself. I drew a stuttered breath. All he wore was a bow tie and Chanel for men. He glinted a smile. He was massive. Eyes wide, I didn't know if he could "fit" inside me.

He reached out, pulling me into bed.

"You wore your scent," he whispered into my shoulder, tasting my flesh.

"I did," I said, tonguing his lips.

We kissed long and hard, exploring each other like the blind with our hands, melding our bodies with love-sweat likened to making up centuries of unrequited wants. The temperature of the room rose. Pools of sweat gathered between us.

"This is intense," he breathed.

"I need water." I giggled.

As he rose from the bed to turn on the air conditioning, I drew a breath. His body was magnificent, gleaming in the dark shades of the lightly drawn curtained room. I could make out every inch of his divine trunk muscles, his rugged jaw and gladiator toned legs. My clitora ached, she was hard. He drew ice from the small bucket, poured the raspberry vodka, swirled, and sampled to see if it was cold enough. He slid back into bed.

"Drink, you'll like it," he said, gently raising the glass to my lips.

It was superb, we shared it to the last clump of ice, when he pulled me on top of him, rubbing my outside sanctum till it flushed with erotic oil. The glass fell onto the floor. He slid down, exploring my belly, covering it with gentle kisses, caressing my breasts with his fingers. My eyes spontaneously closed, and I could feel his engorged-weapon hard-pressed against my calves. His breaths were coming heavier as he worked his way to the glistening isle of Shangri-la. "Open sesame," he breathed, preening the inside of my thigh. I splayed my legs ever so smoothly. The captain of my heart dove into the abyss, found the pearl to my gate, and worshiped it with his magical tongue. I writhed in copious ecstasy, held his ears steady, guiding his momentum.

Blindly panting, lost to the world, our blood boiled its rapt hormones, scorching our minds and bodies. We were out of control, nothing was sacred. Ready to be one.

Reginald mounted me, his glistening ebony erection resting between my legs.

"I want to release myself in you," he breathed, face flushed, guiding himself just in front of my ivory *arcata*.

Just then his iPhone went off. It was Philomena's ring tone -"At last." I'd heard it many times before.

Fuck. I rolled my eyes, my face channeling snicked purpled hues.

"Shit, I've got to answer that." He rolled off and grabbed his phone, his penis throbbing uncontrollably. He answered the call, panting heavily. It was obvious he was breathless.

I could hear her little girl choir voice panging for attention between his "Yes, honey, I'm fine, just ran to answer your call. No, really, I'm fine. No worries. I don't need a doctor cupcake. Yes love, I will. I'll meet you at my apartment right after my last class. I love you forever, too."

It pissed me off. Made me sick. When he was finally off the phone, I sidelined him a stink-eye.

"I'm sorry babe, you know my situation."

The whiny bitch had made him go flaccid. Nevertheless, we were now undisturbed.

"Come here," he said, winking. He reached across me, grabbing the glass of the tinted vodka.

He poured it leisurely into my belly button, swirled it around with his finger, leaned in and drank of its essence. His other finger flirted with and buffed my glassed pearl as he swelled back to life. His curved black shaft stretched over his entire belly. I slid down, licking, tasting, sucking and drank his escaping pearls. The sedulous anticipation made me shudder.

I was vulnerable to the core, powerfully addicted to him. I surrendered myself, body, and soul. Our bodies moist, he slid on top of me. We caught each other's eyes, an intense stare into each other's soul window. I found my hero.

My legs curled around his hips, wrapping themselves in an obsessive hold, awaiting the triumphant "P." I felt his powerful energy surge into me. I surrendered my power, blindly letting him take and conquer my forbidden valle de sanctum. I was lost in his arms, his sorcery, his seduction. I squeezed my muscles, wanting to take him deeper and deeper into the mysticism of love. I had no shame in what I did. I cast my eyes down between the crack of our sweating bellies, watching his long glistening black shaft move in and out of my ivory arcata. Our bodies wrestled like animals, tied together for hours, at times grinding furiously, then followed by tender merges.

"Reg, I'm so in love with you it hurts," I whimpered between fiery kisses.

"I'm mad about you Lucretia. You're on my mind every moment. I swear it."

He lifted my legs over his shoulders, closed his eyes, grit his teeth, and thrust himself deep inside me. His lips contorted as he released, pulsing his fulgent string-of-pearls within. I quivered as I felt the flood of his gloss purl out my lushy, warm, slick, and wet. He didn't pull out, staying rooted and granite hard. My clitora was on fire as he drew sensual circles round it with his pubis, his penis still bedded in conquest. It didn't take long. When I reached orgasm, my mind took me to another place, the place of where the gods of sex dwell. I saw stars in another realm. My calves, feet and jaw seized, locked in painful ecstasy.

We were in free-fall, truly enamored with each other. We were joined in the universal experience of a man and woman. He held me close, whispering adorations.

"I love you Lucretia," he murmured.

"I love you too, Reg."

Satiated, we fell back, exhausted. We slumbered in each other's arms for hours.

Philomena

Click…click…tung! Someone was jiggling the room lock. The door creaked open, letting in the hallway light.

My eyes shot wide open.

The hotel receptionist had let herself in "Room service!" she quipped. The woman's skirt lips cracked a dry smile as she held the door wide open.

A skinny red-head burst balls- out into the room.

"You vile fuck!" She screamed.

Reginald's face ghosted.

"Philomena-"

"I'll be going now," sneered the clerk. She closed the door abruptly.

"Do you think I don't know what you do on Thursdays? You fuck! The University told me Thursdays are your days off." Rambling curses, she tramped back and forth in front of the door, perspiration running her hairline.

"I've had you followed for weeks." Hatred poured from every cell of her body.

I drew the covers, hiding my nakedness.

Reginald jumped from the bed. Not thinking, he approached her stark nude.

"Philomena-" He tried pleading.

Philomena noticed the sex-burns on his penis. Raging, she grabbed the feast basket and threw it at him. He ducked. She reached into her shoulder bag. Before he could approach her, she drew a small silver pistol. Shaking, she aimed it at him.

"I won't be humiliated in front of my society you philandering asshole."

He splayed his palms in a protective stance. "Philomena, no!"

She fired a shot into his upper right chest.

I let out a blood curdling "Murder, murder!"

Reginald grabbed his chest, gurgled, and slumped on the floor.

"I've taught this fucking prick a lesson. He'll live, maimed, but he'll live." She turned. "And you whore. Crime of passion. My family has money."

"Philomena, please, think of your future-" I begged.

Without hesitating, Philomena fired a shot which hit my lower left shoulder.

Breathless, I clutched my crucifix and prayed. "Holy father who art-"

Philomena stepped closer. I could see the menacing, glinting bullet in the barrel. She fired a shot between my brows.

The Last Temple

Philomena blew on the barrel, tucked the pistol into her purse and waltzed out.

Cold Death walked into the room.

Outside, the winds came.

The fireplace crackled as icy drafts swept through the room.

Lucretia was in funnel, twirling with shafts of prismatic lights and flashing scenes of her life. People were motioning, calling to her. Stillness, then nothingness.

Ghosted blackness.

When the last ember from the fireplace died, Father Christoph strode from the mysterious blear rising from the smoke. Staring at the downed orphan's body he had guided and loved through their short time together; he raised his hand. Blessing her tenderly, he whispered the extreme unction.

Together, their souls ascended to the Temple of Eternal Repose.

27   Mexican Phantsy

A Mestizo Autumn

October 17, 2000,   9:45am.

Blonde Mafia

T he Mafia caught glimpses of a young boy and the patrons of abuela Conchita's restaurant scatter as they riddled it with bullets with their AK 47's. They breathed blood.

Inside, the establishment smelled like hot iron, gunpowder and lapsed ripe flesh. There were numerous bloody footprints over checkered black and white tiles, customers that never made it out.

Abuela's last feat, "Corre Miguelito!" was tossing him a steel recipe box and an old deed tied with a leather strap. Her words churned in his mind as he ran and ran, stumbled, and ran. Slithering beneath a wagon painted with the letters, <u>La Rueda Rojo,</u> he quietly sobbed. His head hurt.

The beater Cadillac, with a scythe hood ornament, drove off loaded with automatic weapons, cocaine, and five stocky men wearing dark sunglasses, thick gold pinky rings, and black double- breasted coats.

Miguel Salamanca's chubby fingers swiped away the spiderwebs and dust from the spokes of the wagon he was wedged under. With the cuff of his shirt, he dabbed his tears, hoping to see abuela in the doorway. He was careful not to ruin the deed or roll over abuela's treasured recipe box which he had tucked at his side. Through the spokes of the wheel, he spotted the soles of her huaraches. They were still. And so was she.

Two years earlier

July Summer of 1998

Three American university students from San Diego, who Conchita christened *Los Gringos*, whose passion was Marlin fishing, had discovered her restaurant where they became regulars, feasting on her famous fish tacos.

The location was a lazy beachfront, where the tides lapped gently, the sand forever warm and where the sea yielded plenty of fish for the taking. On certain months, the moon appeared to take up the sky, gleaming the color of golden corn within a fiery crown of hot blue. It was easy to unwind at Conchita's, away from the grunge of the big city, where an ice-cold beer, colorful rattan furniture and warm smiles welcomed one every time. Often, classical Mexican music drifted through the restaurant, all the way to the shoreline at times where Miguel's favorite piece, "Huapango," frequently played; reminding him of his ancestors, talented, strong, and wise.

The gringos lovingly named Miguel Oso, because he was coppery-brown and big for his age of sixteen. Forever in the kitchen, Miguel conjured exotic seaside dishes for their palettes when they came. The gringos looked forward to the summery breezes, the sun-kissed coast, and the aroma of fresh grilled fish smothered with sweet peppery mango salsa. Miguel and Conchita's cheery faces welcomed them each time they pulled up in Kristen's black Jeep. A pitcher of icy Margaritas aside glasses rimmed in coarse salt awaited them the first weekend of each month. The gifts they collected for Miguel during their world travels; odd cooking pots, gadgets and unique utensils fascinated him. He asked tons of questions about the countries they visited and how to use the exotic tools.

Miguel often took Kristen Bach, one of the gringos, whose discipline was archeology, hiking on a path behind the restaurant into the jungle. It led to a site where an ancient civilization of unknown origin once existed. No one knew of its whereabouts, except Miguel. Kristen's thesis on the site would lead her to attain her dream of a Ph.D. and earning the distinction of Summa Cum Laude.

"Kristen, today, we go to a sacred place. Where magic herbs grow," said Miguel, lips curling wide.

"I'd love that! Todd and Brett won't be able to join us. They left for an early dive. We'll see them at dinner."

"Aye no. I was hoping they'd enjoy the hike."

"They're not much for hiking, they're the fishing and diving kind. Let me get my boots and equipment. Then we'll vamoose. I think we can drive halfway, right?"

"Si Senorita, you should wear long pants. I have a machete you can use. We're going deep in the jungle."

"Si, Capitan," she said, winking. "Well noted. I'll be ready in ten."

Miguel was leaning on the Jeep with two machetes by his side when Kristen arrived. Readied for the dense jungle, he wore a loose cotton shirt embroidered with a hand stitched sheaf of wheat, a charro leather belt with a tiny silver star, drawstring brown cotton pants and sturdy leather huaraches.

"Vamanos," she said.

Kristen was in awe traversing the jungle, bumping along the root tangled roads. She listened to Miguel's stories; his ancestors of mixed blood and of the hidden cenotes of torture and the magic he would soon take her to.

They stopped the Jeep where the road abruptly ended. Then it was on foot. The sightings of beaded green, scarlet, and banded iguanas, slithering amongst the palms with their curious rolling eyelids made for excellent video. She stopped frequently to photograph the curious beasts.

"Kristen," Miguel pointed. "My garden."

"Oy!" she said, taken back by the striking colorful herbs.

"And this one," he said, kneeling on an algae-soddened log. He gingerly plucked the nettled top off a scarlet-tipped herb, growing on the edge of the log. "A mix of Mayan and Aztec plant."

"What?"

"I cut and tied the plants together como the Mayans and Aztecs did in their drawings. The red goo makes wrinkles go away. Abuela smears the goo all over on her face to chase away the worry marks."

"Say that again?" asked Kristen, recalling how extraordinarily young-looking Conchita was for her age. She knelt beside him, studying the flame-colored plant. She sniffed the red tip which smelled like a blend of honeysuckle and pear cactus. She raised her eyes from the nettle. "This is remarkable."

"Si." He sprinkled the nettles in her hand. "I dry the hairy parts in the sun and crush them with a molcajete, then I mix with aloe to make a cream.

"What do you call that mixture?"

"I don't know Senorita. Magic goo. That's what abuela calls it."

"I absolutely must catalogue these herbs. May I take some clippings? I would like to send them to my father's lab for study."

"Oh si. Take as much as you want for your Papa," he said, mesmerized by the way her moon-gold hair glinted in the sun. Not only was she beautiful she was magic too, he thought.

Kristen pulled out a zip-lock bag and tucked the samples into her backpack. They furthered deeper into the jungle, looking for remnants of lost civilizations.

What amazed Kristen was a stone altar that she and Miguel had discovered while exploring. Her foot had caught a tangle of vines. When Miguel hacked the tangles, an ancient altar unmasked itself.

"Would you mind if we removed the vines, so I can photograph the altar?"

"Si, no problem Kristen. I am happy to help with your studies."

Later that afternoon, Kristen, Todd, Brett, and Miguel were hacking off the vines, exposing the two-thousand-year-old treasure.

On their second summer visit to Conchita's, the day of the solstice, Todd proposed to Kristin atop the curious alter in witness of the whole *mishpocha,*

friends. Afterwards, abuela Conchita prepared a feast of steamed fish wrapped in banana leaves, fresh salsa verde, sopa de arroz, sopes filled with spicy chicken, beans de la olla, tortillas de mano and for dessert, marinas de leche. The tequila and limes were plentiful that evening.

Even Miguel was allowed a shot.

"My dreams are to be a Mexican chef, and I will open my doors to the hungry and teach them how to cook," he said, beaming a toothy smile." Food makes people happy. Abuela has promised me her recipes."

"And you will, Oso." Kristin smiled. "This is the best Mexican food I've ever had," she said with a spoonful of rice in her mouth. "You and abuela should open a restaurant in Los Angeles. You would rock!" She turned to her fiancé. "In America, anything is possible!"

"Dude, serious, you ought to consider what she said. This food is fabulous," said Todd, nodding his head in agreement. He reached for two warm corn tortillas filled with tilapia, chopped cabbage and pico de gallo. He sauced them with a chipotle drizzle and finished dressing it with a squeeze of lime.

"Stands alone," said Brett, savoring a soup of the sea.

"Amigos, a toast to your engagement…" hummed Conchita, setting down a round of five jiggers of blue agave tequila, lime wedges, and a small bowl of coarse salt. "Mexican style."

Todd dipped his fingers into the bowl and sprinkled the salt on the back of his hand.

"Andale!" goaded Conchita.

Todd licked the salt, bit the lime, and swiftly downed the tequila. He threw his head back and let the Aztec ceremony bedazzle him. He smacked the empty jigger down. "Smooth…"

"Now…" Conchita twiddled her fingers over the rest of the rounds.

Everyone happily obliged.

"My ancestors have been farming this land for many years, growing the spices brought by the Spaniards and from the Mayas on the Caribe side. They knew the mysteries of all the plants of this world. We are lucky to remember their teachings."

"You certainly learned from them," said Kristen, dribbling salsa onto her taco. "Oso, I've something for you here," she said, rummaging through her backpack. She pulled out an elongated black velvet box with a tiny silver bow atop. "For you."

His eyes widened. "For me? Aye Senorita," he said. He gently unraveled the silver ribbon, heedfully opening the mystery box. His breath caught. A most unique golden spoon inscribed with his initials glittered on a chain of gold. "Dios mio!" He swiped the tears from his eyes with the back of his hand.

"Made especially for you. You've helped me tremendously with my studies." She rose, giving him a warm hug.

"Dios, Kristen. Thank you. I have never owned such a beautiful piece," said Miguel, profoundly grateful.

"Mijo let me help you. Turn around," said Conchita, lifting her plump bark-colored arms. She fastened the gleaming pendant around his neck. "Que rico. Gracias Kristen," she said, then went about making her tortillas.

"Kristen tells me that you grow all the spices for the restaurant. That's awesome," said Todd.

"I read the books from the town's library, and I've collected old clay pots written in Mayan, and the Spanish books, I understand," he said, proudly. "Our guacamole is classico, because of Abuela's *aguacate* farm," he said, pointing to a southern facing window. "Good land, which the bad men have been wanting for a long time. They've offered us a lot of money."

"Miguelito! Silencio!" blurted abuela from across the room while her pudgy hands rolled the kneaded flour masa into soft little pillows. Pupils dilated; she scanned the room to see if any patrons caught wind of his babble.

Miguel, red-faced lowered his eyes. "But no, we're happy and blessed. We'll never sell it. Abuela said she will pass it on to me. Si abuela?"

"That's right mijo, we'll never sell." Ruffled, she eyed the gringos body language for their response. When the last of the patrons left, she finished toasting the tortillas and approached their table. "The Mafia needs my land to move their drugs, un routa directamente," she sighed.

"Damn. How long have they been hitting you up?" blurted Todd.

"Are you all right here? I mean, that's the Mafia," said Kristen.

"We are, they've been coming for years. I give them what I can. I do not understand their language or why they all have moon-colored hair. The son of the leader comes here with chains of gold around his skinny neck, cocking like a rooster. His front tooth glitters con un symbol. Aye dios mio he looks so foolish." She rolled her eyes and cleaned the masa off on an apron of faded sunflowers. "We don't make much. But they know I always pay. I think that clown is full of bean winds," she said, snickering. "As long as I put a plate of food in front of him and I give him money, he leaves us alone. Blue-eyed diablo." She gestured a backhand wave.

"Maybe you should buy protection, a gun. Something," said Kristen.

"No, senorita, no violence, no guns. It's a way of life here for people who own something. One day these men will tire of me saying no. They're harmless if I keep paying."

"But abuela, they're not harmless. You told me they killed abuelo because he didn't give them money," piped Miguel.

Kristen opened her mouth to say something. There was an unnatural stillness within her. Instead, she lifted a brow and shot Todd a grim look.

October 17, 2000, 11:45am

Iron Cross

Miguel inched his way from beneath the wagon after the Mafia had long been gone. Somber faced, he dragged abuela's body to the back of the restaurant, grabbed a shovel, and put her in the ground. Ten minutes later, he fastened an iron cross and stilted it over her grave. *What have we done Dios for this to happen? What am I going to do?* After pondering over her gravesite for hours, he reached a conclusion. He would have to leave his land forever. The Mafia would soon take over it for smuggling drugs. It wouldn't be easy leaving Mexico. Frightened, he rose and etched her name into a crude piece of nearby wood. He made the Sign of the Cross over her grave. And blessed himself too.

The back room where Miguel slept was furnished with a wooden bed box, hand-made by his abuelo when he and his mother moved in. It was dressed in sheets fashioned by flour sacks stitched together, freshened, and whitened by the sun. There was a bookcase the gringos had gifted him with, teeming with various books on cooking, spices and how to prepare the dishes of the tropics. A picture of his mother, Mari Luz Xochimil Salamanca, who had crept off years ago, was nailed above his bed with a crucifix beneath. A small window with a jarrito made of terracotta clay rested on the ledge that abuela kept filled with well-water, so that the sun could marry the spirit of clay into the water.

    Miguel's eyes lingered on his books. He wept, grateful to have drunk in much of their wisdom. He would have to leave them behind, but still had abuela's recipe box which he kept clutching for comfort. While stuffing his backpack with light clothing, seeds, abuela's deed and recipe box and two bottles of water, he thought about what Kristen had said, *In America, anything is possible.* He had no relatives or friends there. He knew Kristen was from San Diego but dared not bring her his Mafia troubles. He had become a man now and was on his own.

He plucked his mother's palm straw hat hanging from a nail behind the door, threw his serape over his head, hoisted his backpack over his shoulders and headed for the dusty roads of Mexico.

Miguel hailed down Tito, the ironworks man, who was making a delivery to Tijuana.

"Where to?" asked Tito with a show of bad water-tainted teeth.

"Can you take me to San Ysidro?" He feigned a smile, silent lipped about what had happened.

"Si, hop in the bed," said Tito gesturing over a stack of iron-scrolls resting on the passenger seat. Tito thought nothing of seeing Miguel hitchhiking as he frequently did so when he needed to go into town.

Miguel crammed himself into the back of Tito's open truck which was filled with wrought iron gates and bird cages. The main road was devilishly pitted, the ride bumpy and rough. Miguel had to double tie his hat to keep it from flying away. The truck turned onto the main highway to Tijuana. Fields of corn, wheat, beans, lettuce, and onions raced by in blurs of color. Wafts of cabbage, cilantro, and the sharp nip of onions, ready to be harvested, fashed his nose. To the east of the vegetable fields, the high sierras gleamed in the sun. West of the highway, avocado trees ripe with fruit brought to his mind the situation of what was to be. He pulled his straw hat down over his eyes, they were too painful to look at.

Tito dropped him off nearby the San Ysidro border. "Go with god, Miguel," he said, sun- burnt face crinkling in the sun. He tossed Miguel an orange.

"Gracias Tito."

Slauson Avenue

Vendors selling clay pots, pinatas, striped blankets and colorful ponchos lined the main street. Tourist's kids were having their picture taken on a tired striped donkey with long eyelashes, swatting away time with his tail. Nearby, a street vendor was making chorizo tacos which smelled delicious.

Miguel headed toward the truck stop. It was busy with truckers fueling, eating, and trading stories. He sauntered about, pretending to use the dirty pay phone outside the snack shack. He sat, drank his water, and listened to the truckers' jaw about where they were headed. One trucker with a heavy Spanish accent was talking about returning home to Los Angeles after being on the road for two weeks. He was lamenting how much he missed his family. It was this man he followed unnoticed to a discolored truck, tricked out with clique graffiti. A sign on either side of the truck read GENERAL COAST in black letters. He sat nearby on an abandoned tire, ate his orange while keeping an intent eye on the truck. In that late afternoon he wedged himself under the man's semi, pulled his serape unto himself and prayed for grace.

Two lanes away, a shooting ruckus broke out, distracting the border authorities who waved Miguel's freedom truck through.

The truck stopped several times to refuel. The diesel fumes nauseated Miguel, who wheezed, choked, and had to cover his mouth and nose to escape the noxious fumes that kept inflaming his lungs. During the long ride, he thought about how he would support himself. The people in his barrio had said there were plenty of opportunities; selling oranges, flowers, or gifts from big street corners to start out. Maybe even get a job in a restaurant cooking abuela's famous tacos.

Somewhere in Los Angeles County on a street called Slauson Avenue, the truck pulled into a parking lot. Miguel's ears perked. The radio faded; the vibrations stopped. A door squeaked from the cab, followed by the plop of a leather bag onto the asphalt turned Miguel's head. Two pointy cowboy boots thumped the ground. From a short distance a door slammed, a woman's and children's voices chippered. A pattering of feet, then a man's greeting. There was such joy in the voices. The trucker's last stop.

After hearing car doors slam, and the far away crunching of tires on gravel, a rueful Miguel untied himself, placed his hat and set afoot. It was cold. Every breath he took curled to steam. He talked aloud, repeatedly telling himself everything would be all right. But his face still sagged beneath his hat. The stitching of his left shoe had come apart after walking for over an hour and a blister on his toe had burst. He was careful to keep low and ducked behind parked cars when others passed. It was after midnight. Exhausted, he needed sleep. A sign on a bridge ahead read Montebello. Below it was a dry riverbed scattered with runoff debris. He floundered halfway down the incline, holding on to his shifting backpack. The loose dirt almost sent him tumbling. The moon had dimmed, making it difficult for him to see, but he was able to crawl just below the overhang. It was cold, dank, and smelt of damp rocks and pee. The space was tight, but he was able to shimmy nigh the concrete juncture. It was difficult, but he managed to wrap his serape around himself. And it seemed the rain was coming, but nevertheless he was able to drift off to sleep.

Thunk. Thunk.

Miguel lifted his head, blinking away the sleep.

"Hey! What are you doing up there?" A woman squealed from below holding a handful of dirt rocks.

The sun had burned off the marine layer. It was a big-bellied gringa on a bike with crunchy yellow hair that spouted from under a pin-striped hat. Smokey the Bear earrings hung from her droopy lobes, and her butt was smothering the seat. She was searching her back pockets for something. Silent, he didn't move.

"Damn wettie, you don't belong here," she shouted from two yellow buck teeth. "I'm calling ICE." She rode off cussing.

Miguel righted himself, trembling. The Santa Ana's were howling cold. He double knotted his hat to stay put and bolted from under the bridge.

Beverly Blvd, the sign said. He tucked his arms beneath his serape and headed north, all-the-while in fear of his illegality.

"You! Wettie! Go stand with your cousins at the Home Stop." Three guys snarked, honking from a passing car. The car rolled to a stop. One guy with a nose piercing jumped from the car with a fish bat in his hand. He came at Miguel, bashing his arms, clobbering his back numerous times.

"Fockin' wettie." He grabbed Miguel's backpack, unzipped it, and threw its contents onto someone's front lawn with some of it scattering into the street. He broke into laughter.

"Adios! Go back to where you belong." The guy shouted jumping back into the car.

The other brawler gunned the engine. They took off, wheels screeching, running over Abuela's recipe box.

"Get off my lawn!" An irate old man yelled from behind a screen door.

A flood of humiliation rushed Miguel. *Their hatred was real.*

He swallowed his sobs while gathering the recipes which were blowing into the street and onto the lawn, at which the homeowner had turned the sprinklers on to shoo him away.

Cheeks burning, he wanted to fade into the background so no one would notice him. He wouldn't leave till every recipe was accounted for. He looked up to Heaven and blessed himself when he picked up the recipe box. It was still salvageable.

Trotting the road, he spotted a JoJo's Burgers. Famished, pride no longer existed. He shuffled to the eatery's stone bench, picked up a discarded newspaper to hide the blows and pretended to read. He waited for a few patrons to leave, then pounced on their leftovers.

A tall young woman, with eyes and hair like black silk, had noticed the lone boy crying behind a newspaper. For some time, she had eyed him grabbing scants of leftover food, even devouring the customer's picked out onions. The boy's face was swollen with mottled purple spots. She whispered to her husband. He looked over at Miguel and nodded. The beauty rose and approached Miguel.

"Do you need help?" she said, widening her deep black eyes. "I am Elda." She touched his arm. "You are hungry."

Miguel looked up at the woman towering over him who resembled a Mayan princess. She wore a dark blue snug dress that matched her round earrings of lapis and silver. Her mercifulness was all too whelming. The shame of his male vulnerability pushed him to the edge. He broke into a river of tears.

"Please, don't cry. We're going to talk." She gently patted his shoulder. "Wait here, I'm getting you something to eat."

"Gracias," he said weakly.

"Francisco," she called, waving a beckoning finger. "Come here."

A sobbing Miguel kept his head down, staring at the gang signs etched into the table. His ears were buzzing so strange.. He heard Huapango playing. He shook his head and carved a hand through his hair, holding it back, then released it. Abuela's voice was coming in whispers. *Tell them mijo, tell them. The Spirits tell me they are good people.*

Francisco Moreno hoisted his skinny frame with his cane. Leaning heavily, he tottered over to the boy. He plunked down, smiling subtly. "I'm Francisco."

Miguel's eyes lifted from the table to see an extraordinarily handsome, but becrippled man. "Mucho gusto senor, soy Miguel."

After a long wait, Elda returned with a salad, a burger, french fries and orange juice, pleased to see the boy conversing with Francisco. She seated herself next to her husband and sipped her coffee.

"Tell them mijo. Tell them"… Abuela's voice faded away.

Between tears, shame, and hungry bites he told Francisco and Elda everything.

Lost Dishes of the Americas

Francisco hired Miguel to help around the shop. The decision was easy to make. It would ease his load and aid the young man with attaining a work visa.

Francisco and Elda lived in a modest home in the San Gabriel Valley. They owned a repair shop in Montebello which earned them a viable living. Miguel was a godsend both in Francisco's shop and in the kitchen. Many a day they listened to Miguel's dream of becoming a chef and encouraged him every step of the way.

After Miguel had been with the Moreno's for several months, Elda effectuated an idea that had been stirring for months. She sectioned off a wide patch in their backyard that was rich in brown soil.

"This is where you will grow your magic herbs," she said, handing him a trowel. 'Your seeds will do well in the California sun."

The garden had a positive effect on Miguel and with each till in the garden, he took on a brighter outlook. His pudgy face lit more.

Miguel took great delight in creating the lost dishes of the Mayan, Zapote, and Yaqui Indians for the Morenos and for their neighbors who regularly bought from him. He occasionally threw in a savory tortilla Espanola with onions, and jamon empanadas which everyone raved about.

"Miguel, you must stay low during these times. You still do not have your papers, but I'm working hard for you on them. They are expensive. Soon," said Francisco.

December 18, 2000

A Mestizo's Winter

Kristen's Jeep swung into the parking lot of La Rueda Rojo, everyone eager to give Oso promising news and his Christmas presents.

The parking lot was empty, except for a few brittle tumble weeds stuck on a fence. Todd rolled down the window. The front of the restaurant was graffitied, and the windows boarded up. Eerily deserted.

"What the hell?" said Todd, baffled. "Stop the motor."

Todd and Brett jumped from the Jeep, their eyes scanning from the restaurant to the shoreline. All that was sounding was bustling winds, seagulls harping and the roaring of high tide.

Todd turned to Kristen, "Wait here till I call you."

She nodded, crimping her hands, biting her lip.

"I'm going out back to see if I can look inside," said Brett.

Todd stood, shuddering in a pool of dried blood at the restaurant's boarded door. He kicked apart the decrepit slats, which splintered onto the ground. He peered in. The restaurant was ravished and had been looted. Chairs were busted, plates of half -eaten desiccated food sat waiting for ghost customers on the table. Broken glass and flatware were scattered across the floor, empty glass bottles of cola and cups stained with dried orange drink were still sitting on the counter.

"Back here!" Brett blasted a whistle.

Todd gestured to Kristen to follow him.

A large mound with an iron cross christening its center rested dismally next to a dead tree. Kristen's eyes scanned the words. Scrawled on a dead piece of wood, hedged at the bottom of the tree was the name, "Conchita."

"I am sick," said Kristen, gripping her stomach. "I can't believe this is happening."

"Look," said Brett.

Kristen and Todd riveted.

Brett was standing a few feet away on a gravel road which had recently been laid. "The Mafia is building a route."

"We've got to find Oso!"

"Kristen, if he is here, we'd have known by now. The restaurant has been abandoned for some time. It's boarded up. Looted. There's death here. We can't stay, it's too dangerous," said Todd.

"No, not until we find Oso," she said, probing Todd's eyes for mercy. "I'm begging you."

"Kristen, please. We've got to leave. Just look around." His eyes were wild.

"The fricking Mafia," ranted Brett. "We need to cut bait and blow. They'll be coming back to finish the route. They can't be far."

Todd led an inconsolable Kristen to the jeep.

"We've got to find him Todd. He's told me he goes to Tijuana for food and to visit his friends." Kristen's eyes were rimmed in scarlet.

"Do you know who his friends are?"

"No, he never told me their names."

Todd knew Tijuana was fraught with danger for gringos, especially with the Mafias taking hold of the streets.

Todd relented, repeatedly rubbing his face, and chewing on Tums as he drove into the city of Tijuana where they parked in the Zona Rio district.

They searched the streets for days on end.

Where are you little buddy? It's dangerous here for you, dude. Todd hadn't slept in over forty-eight hours and a virus was beginning to take hold.

"We've got to go. I'm having trouble focusing," said Todd reluctantly.

Fruitless and in deep silence, they headed back to San Diego.

December 28, 2000

The Newspaper Article

"Miguel, your work Visa arrived in today's mail. You are legitimate." Francisco beamed a smile, handing Miguel the document.

"Finally. Gracias!"

"Miguel, Francisco. Look at this."

Elda held up a newspaper article announcing a contest for international cuisine. The prize was ten thousand dollars, but the cuisine had to be original. Miguel had six months to grow the rare herbs that were paramount to perfect his dish.

"You will enter abuela's tacos famosos, si?" cried Francisco, his hazel eyes glistening with excitement.

"Si. I'll be happy to try."

Francisco helped Miguel polish his entry, taking a picture of it with a new cell phone. He uploaded it into a refurbished laptop bought from a neighbor with the money they earned selling Miguel's tacos. Off it went via email.

The wait was torture for Miguel who questioned Francisco for word relentlessly.

The email arrived on a Tuesday morning.

"Miguel. Elda. Look!" yelped Francisco, limping over to them in the kitchen.

"What?" Miguel curled a trembling knuckle against his chin.

"Chico, you won!"

June 30, 2001

A Mestizo's Summer

Dr. Kristen Stein pushed away her routine breakfast of egg whites, half an avocado, strong tea with honey and one slice of wheat toast. She picked up the magazine she had tossed off earlier. And gasped. Miguel's face beamed on the front cover of Cuisine Today magazine. The article read that he was to be presented the prestigious International Chef of the Year award that evening at the Angeles Forum.

The city of Los Angeles was two to three hours without traffic from Coronado Island. Immediately, she grabbed her cell.

"Todd… Todd…It's important you leave your office early," she said breathlessly.

"What's the matter? You ill?" He sensed the jitters through the phone.

"No. We've got to be in Los Angeles this evening."

"What do you mean this evening? I've got a ton of work to do. I've got two clients coming this afternoon for a court case tomorrow."

"I've found Miguel. He's here in the States."

"Miguel? Our Oso? Are you sure?"

"Honey, of course I'm sure. His photo is in Cuisine Today's magazine. He is being presented some sort of prize honor."

Todd choked up. At a loss for words, he blanked; openly staring out the eleventh-floor window of his office.

There was a long pause.

"Todd? Are you there?"

She thought she heard whimpers coming through the line.

"All this time we believed him dead."

"I'll be right home." Todd hung up, wiping the mist off the corners of his eyes.

Kristen put in a call to her father, Dr. Wade Bach, the Founder of the cosmetic company, iSmoothe, of which the family had made millions off its miracle anti-wrinkle crème.

Wade made numerous calls to the board members of his company, who then made calls to the Founder's Arts Center who then contacted the Los Angeles Amphitheater. With only hours left, Kristen was intent on honoring the young man who had made dreams possible.

June 30, 2001   8:30pm

The Awards

"Miguel Salamanca. This is one of the most prestigious' awards in North America. How do you feel about winning this?" The thin mustached host beamed as much as his bald head did.

Miguel straightened the gently worn tweed jacket Elda and Francisco had bartered for the occasion.

"I am honored Senor, truly. God blessed me with my dream." He held back the ready to burst tears. *Men don't do that.* "A beautiful senorita once told me that anything is possible in America."

He lifted his pudgy hand and gave a little wave to Elda and Francisco in the front row.

"And now, your- "

Suddenly, floodlights dimmed. The Forum went dark. What began as soft rolling thrums, intensified into rumbling drums. Elda and Francisco sat captivated, baffled by the strange event. The drumming stopped.

A neon lit platform rose front stage with thirty musician's strings and horns angled at the sky. The musicians sat silent, frozen; resembling a famous work of art, waiting to be awakened by the wave of a magic baton.

Amidst a powerful spotlight, Kristen Stein, Todd Stein, Dr. Wade Bach, and Brett Walker stepped onto the stage.

Miguel did a double take. His mouth fell open.

"Kristen-"

Kristen approached, holding a contract and a sealed envelope. She held out her arms, embracing Oso tight.

"Mazel tov!"

The conductress lifted the gorgeous baton of Maplewood. She held it high for a moment. Silence, except for a solitary runted cough coming from the back of the amphitheater. Everyone waited in anticipation for the moment. She looked left, then right, and nodded to the strings section. She waved the baton over the musicians, as if it were a magical living thing.

The magnificent composition Huapango came to life.

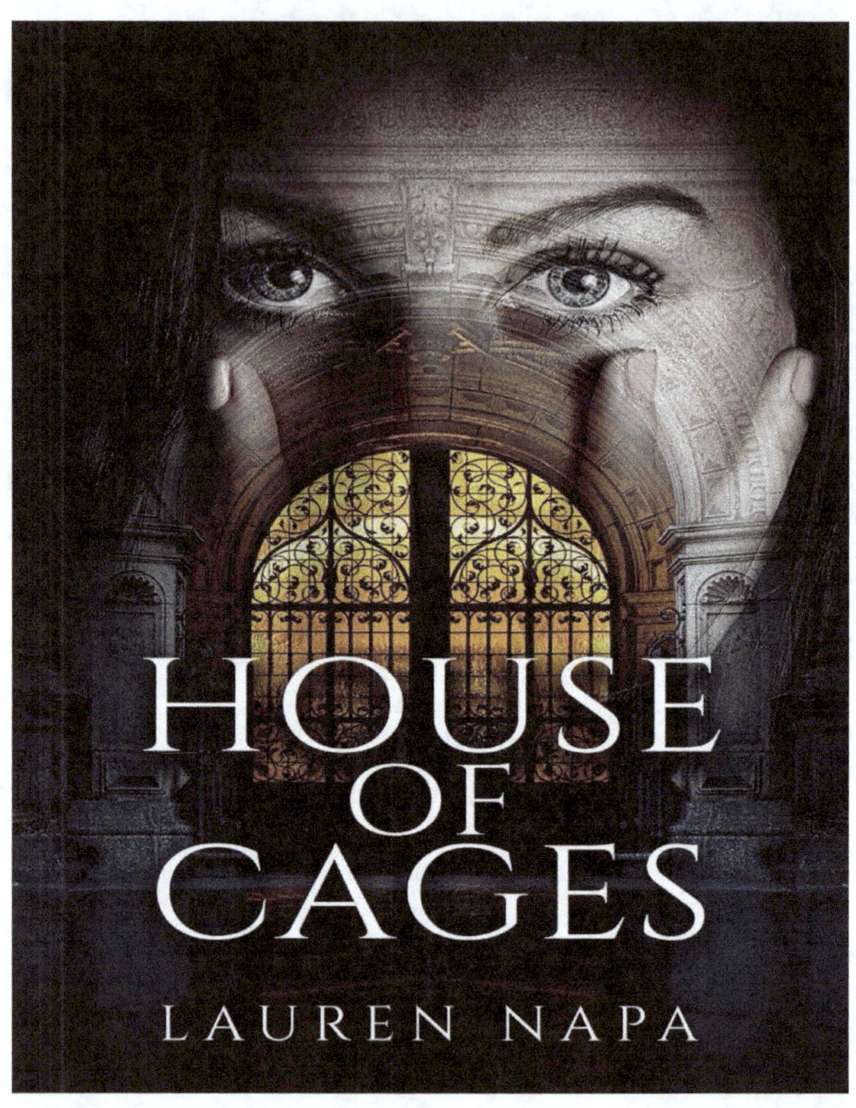

     Mexican Phantsy

THE HOUSE OF CAGES
EXCERPT

On the eve of the Festival of Scorpius, Claret Du Casavant stole her stepmother's clothes and jewelry, and fled the house of cages.

The French Revolution was on the brink of eruption. The more she thought about the *what ifs* she could encounter, the more the hours ticked on in agony. *Soon sisters, soon.*

She had suffered from the torture of a blinding headache throughout the day. Cornelia, her stepmother had the nod of the authorities between her legs and would be harloting her sisters that evening.

"Vous too plain. Les customers complain that you are not easy to look at. You scratch and hit. Just look at yourself. No tits and you are near bald between your legs. You don't bring in as much money as your sisters do." Cornelia reminded her often, as if she had been born an offense. A worthless receptacle for a man's pleasure. A harsh reality of what she had become.

It was a blessing that one of the slow-minded kitchen servants had forgotten about the extra skeleton key in the tea tin before she was dismissed, which Claret had noticed and taken. She would use it when opportune would present itself.

Opportune landed. Cornelia had absentmindedly failed to secure Claret's ankle irons that day.

Cornelia was in the courtyard, primping her chained stepdaughters, sniffing their underarms, and inspecting their teeth as if they were prized horses; ensuring they were presentable to the soldiers. She then led them across cobblestones slickened with after-rain and herded them into a cage.

"Hurry up. Le companies de Marechaussee await you. Monsieur Croix is first. I will service him. He prefers clean. We must not be late," harked Cornelia, voice magnified by the rain-soaked courtyard.

Mounting the carriage, wearing her infamous prostitute hat, she surveyed the area for prowlers. Cracking the whip on Old Molly, she headed toward the stables.

Claret, ensconced aside a window, watched; heart thumping wildly against her ribs, which she thought would crack any moment. She waited till Cornelia passed under the brick arch before she would venture out. They would be gone most of the night. *Soon, sisters soon.*

Returning to her bedchamber, she retrieved the key she had hidden beneath two partially rotten floorboards underneath her bed. After many awkward tries, the ankle irons were released.

Ruminating over the past, migraine still pounding, she wrapped a garter with a pouch around her left thigh. In the pouch were tucked beloved treasures; a deck of worn Naipes cards and a plain gold band with arcane Basque etchings her mother had passed to her on her death bed. "Take care of the Chateau Claret. It has been in my family for generations. You know we are descended from the Divine Ones. Speak the Euskara words when needed," she told her, folding the ring tightly into Claret's palm. Memories of her mother, holding, rotating the gold band by candlelight, and reading it in her ancient tongue of Euskara surfaced. A vague memory also erupted with the Naipes cards. *Was mother speaking to them, or were the cards speaking to her? Mother did it all in secret, away from her father. Hard to be sure.*

She recalled her mother's distress, after fighting her husband's insistence on conferring his family name on the Chateau.

Dismissing the bad memories, Claret trussed a heavy skirt with a cord of buckskin, just enough to fall above her ankles before tying the final knot.

An inner ire would guide her, giving her strength to do what was needed to be done.

Peering out a window, she looked toward the vast moon-cloaked Alps. Gathering her rucksack, she scanned the bedchamber one last time.

Under the veil of night, Claret scuffed along the thorned fence to the stables when suddenly, a hand reached from the bushes and grasped her arm. She swiveled, gasped. Charles, her fiancé silenced her lips with a gentle touch of his finger.

"You frightened me." She raised her palm to her throat.

"Mon amour, I was worried about you. I've been here for a while. You'll need these." He rolled up his sleeves, exposing two muscled arms of scant black curls. He dug into his trousers, retrieving a handful of coins, a strip of cloth and a small dagger in a scabbard.

"Money, a weapon and a cloth; should you need binding."

"Amour, merci," she said setting them down. She dug into her rucksack. "Take this, my mother's wedding ring. Soon to be ours." She blushed. " You can better protect it."

He held the ring up to the moonlight, gently turning and inspecting its perfection. The facets in the flamboyant diamond caromed off his already glimmering pupils. "This ring is worth a fortune." He smiled wide turning to her. "I cannot wait to place it on your finger. It will bind us forever, cherie." He kissed the ring and pocketed it.

Claret took solace in Charles' eyes; avowing the ring to be a symbol of their timeless love.

"I'll ask the ship's Captain to marry us when we're away from this nightmare. France is descending into hell. King Louis refuses to acknowledge the bread riots occurring everywhere," he said taking her hands. "It pains me to see you travel alone. I cannot accompany you. My father threatened me with flogging if I continued to see you. We fought. 'Orrible." He hesitated, pondering a fervor of thoughts. "Should I leave now, my father will suspect foul. He'll show up here, giving your stepmother an earful."

"Oui. I understand."

His soft brown eyes misted. "He called you a putain."

Fire rose in her eyes. "I am not a streetwalker. I was forced into it when my father passed away and she-"

"Shh…mon amour. I know how well Monsieur Du Casavant took care of us. He let us work the vineyards and took on the expenses of our family after my father lost an arm."

"My pe're was a good man. I don't know how he ended up with that excuse of a woman," she said with asperity.

"You should be on your way. Take Rouge, she's wide enough for both of us and fast. Be careful with her, take no chances with injuring her legs," he said rocking slightly. He had a curious concerned look.

"Mon amour. I'm always careful with her."

"We'll meet at the lemon tree before sunrise. That gives us enough time to reach the city, no? We'll set sail from Aubel tomorrow evening for Le Carribe. I've forged our passage documents and readied knapsacks for the journey. The loud of tomorrow's Festival will hide our doings. Careful on the road." He pulled her in and kissed her deep. The taste of her honeyed mouth lingered on his lips.

"I haven't the words to tell you how much you mean to me Claret." He clinched her shoulders. "I love you eterne, mon amour." He embraced her, humming his favorite opera, Bellacosse softly over her nape.

Charles' lips prowled her shoulders. His hands circled the soft berries of her breasts and roamed to her waist. He threw off his belt, his loamy trousers rippling to the ground. Lifting the layers of her skirt, his fingers rimmed the sultry pearl that beckoned him. He grinded the furor of his bulge over her soft mound. Sweat pearled his forehead, his brows, and the palms of his hands. His fingers sought her moist chasm. Breathless, he plunged his urgent passion in and under the big white moon, they made violent love.

Claret surrendered to the madness. She wanted to remain in his arms, to meld with his soul. She felt the fervor of his heart pound against her chest and returned his parting kisses with ardor. Kisses burned in memory.

"Je t'Aime Claret." He pulled a silk auric and royal blue scarf from his pant pocket and dried her goodbye tears. "Keep this. You may need it."

"Je t'Aime Charles," she said with a breaking voice. The sandalwood scent from the scarf brought forth a mesmerizing mix of Charles, love, and piety.

Claret tied the braided scabbard to her right thigh. She gathered the coins and scarf into her rucksack and set off.

As she watched Charles disappear into the night, she walked within his footsteps and caught hints of his earthy sandalwood scent in the backwind.

Thoughts of Chateau Casavant, or the house of cages as Claret ironically called it swirled in her mind.

Pausing her walk, she turned, and saw the deteriorating once graceful Chateau, perched on a terraced hill on the French side of the Alps.

Saddened, she remembered the Perigord walnuts and the private selection of grapes that had been grown in the rich soil of its vineyard that her father was so proud of. Chateau Casavant had been in the family for decades and had provided them with a grandiose living.

All this good life vanished due to her father's gambling and *l'abuse d'alcool,* the curse of liquor which had led to his death. It was a painful remembrance of all that was lost.

The Du Casavant heirs spiraled into grave desperation after Monsieur Du Casavant died. Servants had not been paid for months and had to be dismissed. Angered and bitter, the servants stole all valuable urns, vases, paintings, silverware and statuettes from every floor and chamber, and vanished into the city never to be seen or heard from.

To pay her husband's remaining debts, Cornelia auctioned off their racehorses, except for a decrepit workhorse they called Old Molly, her filly and Rouge, Claret's thoroughbred.

Claret despised Cornelia, a scum who solicited politicians, artists, and poets from café Le Procope. The café being a meeting place Monsieur Du Casavant frequented to discuss political divisions, passions and engage in banter. Cornelia had paid a starving artist to introduce her to Monsieur Du Casavant, then bewitched him shortly after Madame Du Casavant's death. To Claret and her sisters' chagrin, he wed Cornelia during one of his blackouts.

Claret equally despised Caye, Cornelia's Haitian lover, a fetching pirate who had long eyed Chateau Casavant. Witnessing her father, marinated in rum who was oblivious to the lustful moans of Cornelia and Caye writhing in their flesh fests was disgusting.

The hatred she felt for Caye was beyond measure. The nights he would venture into her bed chamber, drunk, trying to penetrate her. She had fought the vulgarian, once blackening his eye, and another time kicking out his dead front tooth. A suspicious Cornelia had beat her after each incident and the beatings became worse as time wore on.

Caye made his move soon after Monsieur Du Casavant died, knowing that the Chateau was worth an immense amount of gold. Claret and her sisters encountered further loss when cock-whipped Cornelia handed over the deed to Chateau Casavant to Caye, who then quickly sailed to Le Carribe with it. The French Courts would never know of its existence.

In exchange Caye would let Cornelia and her stepchildren live in the Chateau to forfend squatters while he was at sea. He also promised Cornelia a pouch of silver each month for food and protection from other pirates and revolutionaries.

It was never Cornelia's right to entrust the Chateau to anyone. Monsieur and Madame Casavant had granted the deed early on to their daughters.

Cornelia resorted to selling her stepdaughter's heirlooms. That's when the cages started to arrive. One, two, three, four, then five. One for each daughter.

Shiny metal cages on wheels with cold iron bars, thick as a jailers. Le bordels they were, rolling brothels.

The path from the house leading to the stables was illuminated by a three-quarters yellow moon which Claret was grateful was not full. The evening was crisp. She passed the garden, equivalent to the mythical gardens of ancient Babylon that framed the west side of the residence where she had once tended exotic herbs and plants. Now it lay in tangled ruins.

Claret fixed her view on the Chateau. She stared momentarily, balling her fists. She turned away.

As she continued to walk, her cumbrous skirt was both a blessing and curse, worth considerably because she had sewn gold and silver coins, hidden from her stepmother, into the hem. Over her shoulders a heavy leather-strapped rucksack held three of Cornelia's lavish gowns.

Tinkles and jingles clinked from the stolen bracelets she had stacked on her wrists, which she repeatedly pushed up her arms. Money barters she could not afford to lose.

After sliding several times on lichen infested stepstones, she bared her teeth, cursing while groping at twisted walnut branches to steady herself. The labor was worth it.

When she arrived aside the barn, she slipped the rucksack off her back and ensconced herself behind a group of water barrels.

While recovering her breath, she reached into her pocket and retrieved Charles' scarf. In the quiet, she brought it to her nose, inhaling the sultry essence of sandalwood. His essence. Closing her eyes, the scent captivated her, immersing her in the promise of love. It would sustain her. Smiling, she tucked it back into her pocket.

Crouching low, Claret glanced left and right, then looked at the moon's bruised face. It was now dark enough to approach the stables.

Through the faint illumination, Claret discerned that the stable's latch was contorted. Shimming it, it did not loosen. She removed her shoe. Pounded it. Still, it did not give. Absorbed, she spat into the latch's give, joggling, and jiggling to straighten it out.

Just then, a blast of whisky fumes shot from behind. She lurched sideways and turned. A hulking Neanderthal with hooded eyes, stained in red was standing before her. She flinched. Two beads of sweat glimmered over his upper lip. A jagged scar that raked his eyebrow spoke volumes. Henri the stable man with the intelligence of a potato was leering at her, his bared chest woolly and moist, rising and falling in anticipation.

"Ah la prostitute! Il est past midnight, no?" He rubbed his hands together.

"Open the stables Henri."

"Pourquoi? Tu run away putain?"

"Bring me Rouge." She grit her teeth.

"C'est le favorite de Madame Cornelia. Ce horse is worth beaucoup money, no?" He raised a bristled eyebrow.

 "Rouge is my horse. My father gave her to me."

"Cornelia et Caye vas a whip me si Rouge is gone." He snuffed, wiping his nose with the back of his hand. "Hmm. If I do, que vas a do for me?" he said face flushing with expectation.

"Bring my horse damn you." She flipped an agitated gesture straight at his nose. "Mount her saddlebags."

"Ah oui putain. Tu monte the horse this time. Rouge no pull your cage." A cruel smile unfurled across his face.

Before she realized, he lunged, trapping her against the stable doors, pawing her in places that should never be touched by a *les miserables*. He reeked of harsh piss.

The cretin knew she would not scream. His drunken hands groped her breasts, twisting and pinching her nipples, his mouth curling lickerishly around her lobes. He pressed against her skirt and chest so hard, she started choking and could not breathe.

Claret tried pushing him off by the shoulders, but he was too strong and continued grinding his rigidness over her petticoat. Too furiously occupied with dry humping her, he did not feel the tongue seeking his ear. Claret's eye tooth clenched his lobe, gouging hard the soft flesh. She wrenched ferociously, ripping off his gold earring.

Henri lunged backwards.

"Beetch! Tu slit mon lobe!" He squealed like a captured hog, bringing his hand to the bleeding ear. Misery creased his face.

"Charles will beat you raw when he finds out you've accosted me." She yanked off a bracelet and flung it at his feet. "Payment for keeping your mouth shut. Now bring my horse," she snapped.

Henri saw the flash of the jeweled bracelet. Still rubbing his ear, he lifted it from the ground. "Vous no tell Charles or Cornelia." He tucked it into his pant pocket. Shaking his head, he disappeared into the stables, cursing.

Claret picked the splinters off her skirt and went to retrieve the rucksack. While bending to adjust the straps for the journey, Henri appeared with Rouge, who commenced snorting and pawing the ground.

"Qu je dit a Cornelia that her horse is gone?"

"That she broke through her confines. Everyone knows this horse has a mind of her own. Lift this across the saddlebags."

"C'est heavy. Q'est in it?" He hoisted the rucksack over the saddlebags.

"No vous business. Help me up."

While helping her into the saddle, he got in a few feels. He felt a hot surge rush into his glutting junk.

"Stop malade."

"Vous a sick fuck too. Adieu putain." He guffawed, dropping his pants. He was stiff as steel.

She upped a stiff middle finger.

Straddled on Rouge, Claret lifted her head and let the cool air brush her face which seemed to quell the daylong headache. She would leave Chateau Casavant behind, well past the greedy eyes of her stepmother. *Never again Cornelia.*

Hope bloomed, thanks to Charles support. As soon as she and Charles would hit the sands of Le Carribe, they would seek the Chateau's deed. It would then be presented to the French Courts.

When she reached the lemon tree of encounter, she looked across the hills. The village was in shadows, except for the faint glowing of burning oil lanterns across the sleeping valley. Tired, she dismounted, guiding Rouge to an adjacent creek to drink.

Leading Rouge to the lemon tree, she swept her hand over the braided mane, whispered soft words, and tied her loosely to the tree.

Charles was late. Inasmuch, she was aware of rumors that bandits haunted the area. He would be cautious.

She wedged the rucksack against the trunk of the tree and curled into a fetal ball. Contented by the thoughts of a future with Charles, she fell asleep and dreamt of citrus blossoms.

When morning came, the breath of the lemon tree woke her. Lifting her head, she blinked away the sleep. Rising, she stretched, then gripped her neck, trying to rub away the knot that had settled in overnight. She glanced over to Rouge. No horse. Only a pile of horse shit.

Color drained from her face. With knuckles clutched tight, white, she darted like a madwoman around the tree, losing her breath and hot-footing down and up the small hill.

"Rouge. Rouge!"

No signs of the horse. Winded, she wept, cursing herself for being such a heavy sleeper.

Scrambling around, she found her rucksack tossed in the briars. Sifting through it, relieved everything was still there. Lifting her skirt, she swiped her hand up her thigh, relieved her garter pouch still held its contents.

Thoughts coming wild, she needed to discern in which direction to head and would need a clear view of the valley. That would be where the lemon tree grew. Trembling, she hastened back.

There hung the frayed rope, thrashing and flailing in the wind. Grasping the unusual oily fibers, she pondered the origin of the oil. She brought it to her nose.

It smelled of sandalwood.

DRIED BRAMBLES

A lurking gloom invaded every bone in Claret's body while making her way down the hill. She wavered between disbelief and hurt, hoping the roiling thoughts were wrong. Torrents of nameless voices followed her. With every footfall, she kept casting piteous glances over her shoulder, searching the road for promise. *He is at the port. Just a mild setback.*

Keeping a steady pace she passed the parish of St. Marie de Olivier; where seminarians were outside praying, and passed a small chicken farm where she stopped and chatted for a short while with a smiling whey-faced woman who gave her two boiled eggs and a wodge of old bread.

A mob of horseflies, drawn by her rankled sweat, soon descended on her like flies on festering meat.

"Oy," she huffed, swatting them.

Flustered by the weight of the rucksack she was hauling and the dull throbbing pain in the balls of her feet, she decided it best to rest for a bit and catch a breath.

She eyed a thicket just beyond a small grove of oaks that sheltered the entrance to a coppice. She brushed aside the plumed leaves and poked her head in. It appeared to be a good retreat and she sauntered in. Spotting a bank of rocks surrounded by soft ferns, it would be a good place to lie still.

Easing down the rucksack, she removed the bracelets from her arms and tucked them into it.

Alone and amongst the pines, she drew in its resinous breath. Her defenses, weakened by a lack of sleep and tiredness, the bad memories of Cornelia and Caye she sought to put an end to, tried to force their way in. She leaned against a faceless tree, slid down and closed her aching eyes. All around unseeable threads of the wind rustled the leaves amongst the trees; drawing in the whispers of the forest.

Soon thereafter amid balmy wafts, came soft drizzles. She rose. Faint trickling coming from behind a copse led her to a thick brier. Parting the prickly leaves, a glinting stream was inviting her to drink. Relief.

While dipping her parched lips, the sounds of clunking wheels, clopping hooves and the strapping of a whinnying horse attracted her attention. It was coming from the road she had just traveled. Careful not to call attention to herself, she minced back to the coppice.

The sun was dominating the west. She squinted between thick foliage to catch a view.

Old Molly and her filly were drawing her caged sisters. At the reins, Cornelia, looking like the prostitute she was, still garbing her ostentatious hat was seated on a tufted cushion, cracking an oiled whip at Henri's bare back as he walked beside them.

"Damn imbecile. Find her and Rouge," belted Cornelia.

Claret, straining to see, accidently snapped a dried branch which flushed out a flock of finch.

"Ecoute? What goes there?" Cornelia halted the horses, bending an ear. She eyed a clutch of bushes just ahead of the carriage.

A cold breath of terror escaped Claret's throat. She held her breath. She looked around, as if a brute would take her there and then. Unwittingly, she clutched her skirt and started bunching it. *I'm going to pee.*

"Nothing Madame. I hear nothing. Un serpent or autre else. Birds fear les serpents, no? La route est full of cre'atures,'" croaked Henri, annoyed at losing time.

"Hmm." Cornelia's forehead wrinkled. "Over in those bushes." She pointed the whip.

A sense of impending doom cast its shadow over Claret. Lifting the hem of her skirt, she blotted the stinging sweat away from her eyes. *Calm down.*

"Si vous think Claret est with Rouge, vou vous wrong Madame. No horse turds. No traces de hooves." Henri coughed up a ball of mucous and spat.

Cornelia pushed a few stray hairs out of her face. A gust of wind rattled a nearby clump of dead brambles. Turning, she eyed the bushes suspiciously.

"C'est calme, Madame. Just le wind. Vous waste time. Les customers expect le femmes soon. Nos losing beaucoup money."

With a hesitant nod Cornelia said, "Very well." She snapped the whip on Old Molly and the wheels churned once again.

Heart pounding her chest, Claret watched the wheels stir up silt on the road; a road taken many times for despicable acts. Letting out a breath, she made the sign of the cross and let her head fall back in prayer. *Soon sisters.*

SEBASTIAN VALENTINI

Claret followed the banks of the River Manette, named for its bitterness, contemplating on reaching Aubel before nightfall. To the east an abundance of bushy thickets lined the road, some dead; rattling in the wind, some alive; vibrant, bursting with wild blackberries on arching canes that reached for the sun.

Her shoulder ached. Her eyes strained, and hunger started to bother her. Luckily, she had had the foresight to pick a handful of berries. *How I wish I had a snort of laudanum.*

Plodding along the road, she heard the clip clops of hoofs from behind.

"Mademoiselle."

She turned.

A beautiful man mounted on a bay-colored horse, wearing a Roman collar, was stopped. He brushed away errant strands of tawny hair where hazel eyes twinkled from beneath gilded brows. He had the longest lashes she'd ever seen. His stare met hers with such force it stunned her.

In silence, their souls collided as if a nova had exploded.

The afternoon was sweltering. The priest's gauzy-like shirt, moist with sweat, clung to every inch of his ribbed chest and arms. If the myths of the gods were true, he certainly was one.

Claret, cheeks, and neck reddened, stared unabashedly at his body.

"Bonne journee. I'm Father Sebastian Valentini."

"Ah, er, enchante Father." A deep flush of heat crept across her ears and face. *Oy vey. Did he see me gaping?* A small awkward curtsy was in order. Dipping her crimsoned face, she fidgeted with the sliding rucksack.

"And you are?" He had noticed her roaming eyes which made him face his boyhood timorousness.

"Claret Du Casavant." A shy smile surfaced.

"Bonjour Claret Du Casavant," he said, followed by a visible swallow. He shifted in the saddle. "Why are you carrying such a large sack in this heat?"

Her mind raced to find answers. "Ah oui, I'm going to visit my uncle in Aubel who has taken ill. My family's carriage broke down several months ago. So here I am." She gesticulated with open palms.

"It's dangerous for you to be out, especially alone on this road. Would you like a ride into the city?"

Claret hesitated, holding a vacant stare not realizing that she was grazing her thumb against her palm. She had no idea how much further or longer she would have to walk. Biting her lip, she leaned slightly to look behind Father Sebastian, focusing her eyes on the road, watching for any sign of Cornelia who would be traveling to different customers today.

"You looking for someone? Is everything alright?"

"Oui, oui Father. Everything is fine. I don't wish to burden you. 'Onest, I can walk," she said in a quiet voice.

"Nonsense. You are god's child. Let me help you. That sack looks heavy."

The priest dismounted and lifted the rucksack off her shoulder. "There now, better, yes?" He placed the sack on the ground and gently rubbed her upper arm and back. When he finished, he flashed her a brilliant smile.

Claret's ears burned red. No stranger had ever been this thoughtful before. *Why? How curious.* Her muscles tightened. Her stomach fluttered. She wanted to run. She cleared her throat and took a deep breath before saying anything.

"Oui. Thank you Father." *Calm yourself stupide.*

"Of course." Sebastian tied the rucksack across the saddlebags and patted the horse.

"Come Claret."

"Un moment Father."

Claret rolled her hair, tucking it into the back of her blouse. Digging her sack for Charles' scarf, she covered her fire-gold hair; which hues recalled the gold eye of heaven, to shield her from recognition.

As he hoisted her, their eyes met again, her violet eyes dazzling in the suns glint. There was a potent sweetness about her which sent powerful waves throughout his body. He startled; his heart quickened. There was tension in his muscles. He felt his vulnerability.

"You good?" he said with a nervous smile.

Claret nodded subtly.

He mounted and gave the horse two short clucks with his tongue, then gave it a gentle squeeze.

"Call me Sebastian," he said with a slight look over his shoulder.

Claret gripped his waist, trusting this man of the cloth. A sense of relief washed over her as she cradled her head into the slope of his back. His solid warm muscles shifted against her cheek. She breathed in the pungent sweet wood scent of his sweat.

The afternoon sun was darkening. They rode through the countryside where carpets of lavender and iris graced the air with their scent, stopping at one point where a sheep herder with a poked-out eye took his time moving bleating sheep across the road.

"Where are you from Claret?"

"I reside at Chateau Casavant. I am the daughter of Francoise Du Casavant."

"You reside at Chateau Casavant?"

Swallowing hard, she hesitated. "Oui." Cringing, at the same time relieved he was unable to see the wince plastered on her face.

Sebastian had heard stories about Chateau Casavant from the curious nuns who took vegetables and bread to the poor. They had been too ashamed to speak wholly of the situation, and of the women who sold their purity to men. Stories that would land them in Hell.

They rode in silence for a long while.

When Sebastian finally spoke, it was of his parish, where it was, the seminarians he taught, the devout parishioners and of his calling.

Claret listened attentively.

The sway of Claret's soft breasts against his flesh, her scent; the scent only a woman gave off, her whisper-soft breaths and the rise and fall of her warm crevice against his lower back was mesmerizing. It was a strong pull. *God, help me resist this enchantress.*

Claret, ashamed, conflicted of how she was responding to the Priest's presence silently asked her guardian angel for help. There was a thickness in her throat. Her knees were weak. She lifted her head and took a deep breath to break the guilt that was overwhelming her.

Father Sebastian's shirt held the sensual blend of man and frankincense; the incense priests used in high mass. It was strange. Being with a holy man who evoked forbidden sensations in her. It brought back her stepmother's branding of her; a whore. In her mind, she believed God sent this priest to help, still holding the deep faith her father had taught her in the early days. Tired, she rested her head once again against his back where the wind cooled her lips and blew the musky scent of his hair at her.

They crossed a rustic bridge where a glassy creek was glittering in the sun's afternoon hues. As she looked into the water, it looked like tiny, brilliant cuts of diamonds. It drew her notice; a theater of shadows was playing out their reflections like lovers with innocent abandon.

"Did you see that?" He twisted his waist to look back at her. "That brook is mischievous."

"It is," she said. *I wish I were that shadow.* Leaning into the curve of his back, she quietly brushed the gauze of his shirt with her lips, scattering two faint kisses.

Sebastian thought he detected soft grazes against his back. *Caresses?* It ignited a long simmering fire that had challenged his calling from the beginning. And disturbed him.

A few puffy clouds drifted by, shading them at times with beams of the sun penetrating through, as if shining their rays on a throne in Eden.

Smiling, she drifted off and dreamt of the allure and temptation of celibate priests. The Roman collar aroused her, sending tingles of pleasure. She pressed her thighs into the saddle, then abruptly woke to a throbbing between her legs. *God, forgive my libertine thoughts.*

"We are nearing the city Mademoiselle."

"Father, could you take me near the port?" she said perspiring, recovering from the dream.

"The port? I thought your uncle ill."

"There's an apothecary there. He needs medicines."

"Of course."

As they passed the fumrie d'opium, she startled; her belly tangled in disbelief. She thought she recognized Rouge's tail braid. Rouge was in a stall blanketed. It appeared that someone was trying to conceal her.

"Stop. Please, let me off here."

"Here? This is an opium den."

"I recognized a friend's horse."

Puzzled, he frowned. And turned his head.

"Your friend habits an opium den?"

"Er, ah. Makes deliveries. I haven't seen him in a while."

At once, Claret slid off the horse and grabbed her rucksack before Sebastian could dismount.

"You sure? I can accompany you." He lowered his head, taking a deliberate hard stare at her.

She cleared her throat. Twice. Then shifted her eyes away.

"I'll be fine." Her voice was stilted.

Sebastian weighed the danger of the situation; a place of heathens, pirates, opportunists, and criminals. He had sensed her naivete, and she was about to enter godless waters.

Claret hoisted the rucksack over her shoulder.

"Last offer," he said with a pained gaze.

"Father I appreciate your concern." She tiptoed and kissed his holy ring. "Merci pour everything." Her voice trailed as she headed toward the opium den.

"Au revoir Claret. God be with you." With a vacant smile, he waved an unseen goodbye. And envied the sun that knew her lips.

THE OPIUM DEN

Claret pushed open the elaborate brass doors of the opium den. Toh Chee, a shrunken ancient man of Asian descent not more than four foot and a half stood at the fore steps welcoming customers. In his hand a dragon carved pipe which he brought to the corner of his mouth. He inhaled and blew out a stream of wicked smelling curls. His face, the color of cherry bark was seamed with hundreds of creases. His reddened half-lidded eyes divulged the use of many years of opium.

"What you like?" he said, probing her eyes.

"I'm looking for a man."

"Fuk, fuk?"

"No, a friend of mine may be here."

"We no run for missing men. You need be customer. If you no smoke or need fuk fuk, you go." He gestured a dismissal wave.

Elegant, he reeked of wealth; the beauty of the robe that graced his bony shoulders, the bejeweled rings on most his fingers and his scented robe said so.

"I will smoke."

"You want smoke? Seven Silvers."

She riffled her sack for coins and handed them to him.

He beamed, tucking them swiftly into his pocket. "You go. Sit there," he said pointing to a bench covered in black and gold velvet. "Song Ling will take you to powders." He strolled to a small gong by the door and hit it twice.

A delicate woman wearing a silken robe embossed with rose petals and orange blossoms materialized. A metal horse clasp between her breasts, forged from pig iron, held her draped gown together. Her facial features were strikingly perfect.

Song Ling lowered her head.

"Girl want smoke. Take her."

"Yes, Toh." Her voice was just above a whisper.

"Leave sack here. We keep safe." Toh inhaled another intoxicating smoke.

"Oui monsieur." Claret offered a weak smile.

Song Ling grasped Claret's hand and led her to a grand parlor where various modes of opium were being dispensed.

Claret looked around the parlor, taking every inch in. Men and women smoking opium, eyeing potential sex partners, beautiful people lounging, being pampered, and rubbed with exotic oils while soft bells tinkled in the background. Nude people on their knees pleasuring one another. Opulence and debauchery. She felt the taint crawling her flesh.

Song ling tugged Claret's arm, breaking the distant spell.

"Girl…Girl! What you name?"

"Oh sorry. Claret. Claret du Casavant."

"That no belong here," said Song Ling pointing to the crucifix Claret was fidgeting with on her neck. "Why you wear?"

"A treasure from my mother. She gave it to me before she died."

"Dead man on wood. So strange." Song Ling shuddered. "What you like smoke?"

"I've never done this before. I would like to go easy, no?"

"Powder of simple pleasures," said Song Ling turning to a dark reedy man standing in front of a grandiose cabinet with eighty niches.

The man retrieved a rolling stepstool from behind a heavy drape and located the powder from atop the highest shelf.

"Pipe or paper?" he asked, stepping off the stool.

"Paper."

He spooned a hefty amount of the brown powder inside a rice paper, expertly mixing it with cannabis leaves and seeds. He rolled it, then handed it to her.

"Is this strong?" asked Claret, rubbing her sweaty palms down the front of her skirt.

"You will like. Smoke slow," she said. *Girl dumb. She not know many things.*

73   Mexican Phantsy

Claret nodded. She followed her instructions and inhaled. A euphoric bliss soon set in.

"We take a walk. We have men who can pleasure you. They come in many colors and creeds. You like a thick root?" she asked, taking her by the arm.

"What?" Claret replied hazily.

Addled with opium, Claret thought she heard a familiar voice as they walked the hallway of the flower pleasure chambers. Stopping, she turned to Song Ling.

"I want to see."

"Oh, you one like watch. More money."

Claret tore a small hole into her hem with her fingernail, fidgeting for coins. She rooted out too many and dropped them into Song Ling's palm.

Song Ling smiled and returned the excess coins. *She young. Not know the world. I have great sorrow for her.*

"We go there. You must stay quiet."

"I know. I want to go to where the music is coming from."

"Yes. It back here."

Through bloodshot eyes, Claret followed Song Ling down the hall. As they approached, the opera, Bellacosse was playing.

"Music beautiful. I like."

Song Ling pulled aside the drapes gently, leaving the underlying veils intact so that Claret's voyeurism could be achieved without being discovered.

Claret's stomach dropped to her feet. There was Charles, grinding, fleshing, pounding a sweaty Cornelia who was on her knees in an oversized bed. His hungry tongue licking and nipping her ear. She moaned and yawped as he punished her with deep plunges. With each hard thrust, her massive breasts swung wildly.

Claret's tortured eyes leered perversely, and she despised herself for it. She recognized the woman lying beside Cornelia as Juliette Salome, the famous opera singer from Aubel.

"Piss off cocotte," Juliette hissed, pushing Charles off Cornelia.

"Je cannot anymore," growled Charles, his glistening shaft throbbing, red and angry.

"Oui, you can," said Juliette.

" 'Orrible beetch." A defeated Cornelia resolved herself to a corner couch, sulking.

It took all of Claret's strength not to rush the insidious orgy. *Cornelia. The opera singer. That's why he was always humming Bellacosse.* Tortured by what she was witnessing, her heart thumped her ears, fingers, chest. She grabbed onto the drapes, almost knocking them down. *How could he? I was so in love with him. He was everything to me.*

Charles deceit was unbelievable. He had shattered her heart. Destroyed her hope.

"You like?" Song Ling whispered. Good yes?"

"No," she said icily.

From the tail of her eye, Song Ling noticed the tears bleeding from Claret's eyes. *Something wrong.*

Livid, Claret waited, coldly, patiently, fingering the dagger against her thigh, forcing herself to face the dark truth. Death would be the only way she could avenge herself. *I will kill him and his cunts.*

Juliette shoved Charles on his back like a huntress, exploring his night-wand with her hungry tongue.

Straddling him, she moved rhythmically, guiding him into her slickened lush mound, leading his hands to her taut nipples, pausing at times to squeeze her warm tight muscles around the gorging iron that was begging for release.

At the mercy of her pleasure chasm, Charles held his strokes, concentrating on holding his stamina.

Claret watched Juliette ride him hard. When Juliette slid her hands up her moist belly slowly under her breasts was when the glint of her mother's wedding ring flashed in Claret's eyes. She uttered a strangled sob and sank to her knees.

"What you do?" Song Ling whispered, lifting her by the underarm.

"Shhh, please." Claret choked out the words, almost forgetting how to breathe.

"We go now," said Song Ling.

"No."

"You sad. We need go."

"I said no."

It took several minutes before Claret could shake off the jolt of what had just happened. When the emotional wave seceded, she peeled apart the drapes, and continued to observe.

Charles turned Juliette on her back, hammering her like an animal.

"I love you Charles. Give me all of you," Juliette belled, digging her nails into his back. She wrapped her legs around his hips, clenching tight his hard root.

Charles could no longer hold the explosive impetus. He shut his eyes, ecstatic stars exploded, and he grinded his teeth and shouted. With a triumphant burst, he let go his seed.

Charles body relaxed while Juliette lay atop, her head resting in the moist conclave of his still-beating chest. She enjoyed listening to the afterglow of his stuttering breaths.

Claret stepped out from behind the veils, fury in her eyes.

"You meant the world to me Charles!" she shouted venomously. The dagger rasped with intent as she withdrew it from the sheath.

Charles, eyes bulging, hurtled off the bed, grasping the sides of his head in panic.. "Claret, let me explain!"

"No!" Song Ling screeched, leaping forward. She grabbed the back of Claret's skirt.

Cornelia turned toward the scuffle. In front of the drapes was a wild looking Claret, dagger in hand ferociously slashing the air. Claret's voice thundered the room. A frantic Song Ling was attempting to grip the dagger. *Shit.*

Cornelia turned to Charles, eyes narrowing. "What does she mean telling you that you meant the world to her?"

"Stop. Stop it!" Juliette was screaming.

Cornelia leapt from the couch. She and Song Ling grabbed Claret's daggered arm and twisted it into submission. Cornelia peeled the dagger from her fingers and threw it on the couch.

"Go find the proprietor. Quick," Cornelia shouted while strong -holding Claret.

Song Ling nodded, making haste. Charles and Juliette scrambled for their clothes.

"Stupid beetch," sneered Cornelia pulling taut a clump of Claret's hair and dragging her to a nearby table. "You're coming back with me; I'll work you harder. You'll never see freedom again."

"Fuck you."

Cornelia leaned over and grabbed a statuette off the table. She struck a heavy blow to Claret's temple. Bone crunched. It sent Claret stumbling onto the floor, rendering her unconscious.

Cornelia looked at Charles and Juliette.

"I'm taking her home. Charles, find Rouge. Come early to the Chateau. You'll take her sisters tomorrow to the mansions."

"What do you mean, ordering him around? He's not your property. Cocotte. Get your own man," hissed Juliette.

"What did you say?"

"Prostituee. You want me to repeat?"

Cornelia raised a brow. "Don't ever call me that again."

"I'll call you whatever I want. You would not have one livre if it weren't for you selling les cunt to Toh's customers and yours to pirates. Truth hurts, no?

C O C O T T E. " Juliette smirked and turned to gather her coat.

Cornelia's nostrils flared. Glaring at Juliette she couldn't contain the surging rage. She seized the dagger from the couch, charging Juliette from behind, plunging it deep into her neck. Blood spurted heavily from the great vein.

"Juliette!" Charles caught her collapse. He tried to stop the bleed with his hands. She went limp in his arms.

"What have you done? Are you mad?" He was slathered in blood.

Cornelia stepped back, ashen looking.

"Elle morte" said Charles, voice cracking, rocking Juliette's body in his arms. "You killed her!"

Cornelia ignored Charles, giving a long pause before responding. Stepping to the blacked-out Claret, she nonchalantly tucked the dagger strategically into her hand.

"She'll hang for that," said Charles hit with nausea. He strained to keep himself together.

Cornelia glazed over Juliette's body. Smirking she turned away.

Hurried footsteps and confused voices were drawing closer from the hall.

On edge, a wild-eyed Charles let go of Juliette's body which slumped to the floor.

Toh bustled in, followed by Song Ling.

"What hell is going here?" Toh lowered his pipe, handing it to Song Ling. Looking down, he stared at Juliette's lifeless eyes.

Everyone quieted. Song Ling blinked rapidly to reaffirm what she was seeing.

Toh circled the bloodied body on the carpet.

"Who kill her?" he blared.

Cornelia pointed to Claret. "Jealous rage. Everyone seen it. See? She still has the dagger in hand."

Toh studied Claret's slow breathing bosom. "Fuk. She out cold. Why she knock out?"

"I hit her before she could attack again." Cornelia's voice dropped to that of an innocent child. She held her stomach. "She is my stepchild and madness runs in her family."

No! Song Ling swept her head in denial. She saw the murk residing in Cornelia's eyes.

Toh folded his arms across his chest. Turning to Song Ling he said," I have no time for this. Summon authority. Take murderer to back room away from customers. Wait for authorities. Be swift."

Song Ling gave a slight nod, then handed Toh back his pipe. She half-lifted a groggy Claret and dragged her out of the room.

"Cornelia." Toh turned, boring his cold black eyes into her and Charles. "You and this pig, rope off room. I send authorities to Chateau for testimony. Get out and no come back." He motioned a nasty gesture.

HENRI

Father Sebastian never left the opium den, keeping a safe distance hidden aside the establishment, intuiting something wasn't right. Claret had seemed so trusting, so innocent, vulnerable. In good conscience, he could not leave her in a place like that alone. He would wait for her to emerge.

Waiting patiently, Sebastian observed the patrons leave. Men were laughing, talking, smoking, smiling, hitting each other on their backs, bragging with the afterglow of sex. An unclean sense crawled his flesh. A bitter tang burgeoned his mouth. He spat it out.

A dull jangle of chains from behind garnered his attention.

A barebacked man swigging the last drops from a whiskey bottle surfaced from the back, goading two young women, clapped in irons, toward a cloaked carriage in front. Stopping, he burped and threw the bottle into the bushes. As they approached the carriage, he yanked the chains to stop. With one muffled swoosh, he removed the carriage's cover. It was a shiny barred cage.

The sisters stepped into the cage as they had done many times, heads down, their hair hanging over their shamed faces.

Father Sebastian slid off his horse and led it to the front while Henri finished locking the cage.

"What are you doing with these women?"

"Saint homme, not your affairs. Go pray for the poor, no?" He sniggered, wiping dirt off the bars.

"You treat them like beasts."

"Help, please help us," came a soft cry from one of the sisters. She gesticulated a begging hand out the cage. The other sobbed and pleaded with silent lips.

Henri turned and stomped his foot. "Tais-toi! You wake le dead."

"Let them go. You're violating these women."

"Les femmes here because they want to be."

"You think I believe that? I'm reporting you to the authorities. You'll be jailed for this."

"No homme."

Henri looked around. There was no one. A dim yellow light from an oil torch was the only witness on the street. Whistling softly, he patted the side of his pants, his hand sliding over the cold iron.

"Por vous." Henri's lips curled to a wily smile. He rapidly drew the iron and fired a shot into Father Sebastian.

Sebastian stumbled back, eyes bulging. He pressed his hands against his side, his crucifix swinging wildly. Blood gushed through the clutched fingers. He swayed, then crumbled to the ground.

"Assassin!" The girl's shrieks snapped the dead air. On their knees, they screeched and rattled the cage like wild captives.

"Shut up, or you die too!" Henri pointed the still smoking pistol at them, kicking dirt into the cage. "Stupids."

He led the priest's horse to the back of the cage, securing it well.

Cornelia, holding onto her ridiculous hat was stepping down the stairs of the establishment when the shots rang out.

"What the hell did you do?" she demanded, looking at the downed man. She came closer.

"Madame, he pose de many questions. He say I go en prison."

"Imbecile! For fucks sakes, he's a priest! We could hang for this." she said, pupils dilated. Her gaze darted the environment, looking for anyone who could possibly be a witness. She paced back and forth, straining to control her breaths. "Behind this building are woods. Drag him there. Oy vey. Do not let anyone see you."

"Yah, yah."

Henri lumbered over and grasped the priest's hands. Dragging him into the woods, he cried while speaking to himself and to his dead mother. *Mere, forgive moi. No prison.*

While dumping the body into a thatch of rotting bogs, an army of crickets commenced their abrades, as if somehow knowing what he had done.

The priest's lifeless expression was tormenting him. He threw mud at the holy face to cover the haunting. *You make me do it! 'Orrible!* The harrow escalated, his breaths started hitching and soon he was in a full-blown panic attack, going in circles. He picked forest debris from the ground and started flogging himself with stems and switches and banged his arms against his side till exhaustion overtook him. He fell to the ground, bawling. *No, mere, no. I sorry. I no go prison.*

When he recovered, he moved the soggy mire to cover the body, stopping frequently to listen for ghosts moving in the forest. Shuddering, he shambled away from the gravesite, covering his tracks by swishing a thick branch.

Pacing back and forth, Cornelia turned to her stepdaughters who were sobbing.

"Not one word of this is to be spoken to anyone. Do you understand me? There will be hell to pay if any of you open your mouths to anyone, including Claret," she said trembling, nervously stroking her throat.

With dulled wet eyes, they shook their heads. "Oui, belle-mere."

Henri returned to Cornelia and the caged girls, grumbling, wearing a scowl furrowed with dirt muck.

"What happened to you imbecile? You look like you've been beaten, no?" Cornelia brazened, laughing at her slap of caste. She fanned away his body odor.

"Nothing, madame." *Femme grossier.* He shot her a rude eye.

"Cover the cage. Walk behind the priest's horse and make sure no harm comes to it. Le horse will bring a good price."

Henri helped her atop the carriage. She took the reins, cracked the whip on old Molly and started back home.

FIERY EYE OF MARS

The back door of the opium den flew open with a loud crash. Song Ling shoved Claret out and tossed her rucksack which landed with a thud.

"I no believe them. Go." She slammed the door. The leaden bolt turned.

Claret's head pounded from the blow Cornelia had thrust upon her earlier. Bringing her hand to her temple, she ran her hands over the dried glob of crust stuck to her hair. Her left eye, purpled and black, had swollen shut. Unsteady, she inched toward the woods behind the den, her body barely being able to sustain its own weight. The swirling behind her eyes was intense and she heaved whatever was left in her stomach. It was difficult to maneuver, and she managed to drag the sack deep into a thick clump of bushes.

The night air was cold and still. Stopping to catch a breath, the scent of copper and iron from her hair were attracting tiny white gnats. The pests busied themselves, whirring and diving into the blood splat on her hair. *Oh god.* She briskly waved them off.

Claret continued to drag the rucksack away from sight where she spotted a great oak. Shucking the rucksack against it, she plopped down on it and listened for a quiet moment to the sweet-winged music of the woods. Laying her head on the sack, her eyes wandered the heavens. She wished what she had been through wasn't true. The pulses in her ears ebbed and weakened, and her eyesight fuzzed with halos. She labored for breaths. The unconscionable night was stealing every ounce of her life.

Stars dimmed on and off in the distance, except for the fiery eye of mars which had made its appearance in the east, watching her quietly making peace with her God.

ABOUT THE AUTHOR

Lauren Napa is a fiction author with a bend toward Fantasy, Horror, Paranormal and Erotica. She has traveled the Mediterranean extensively where she explored its ancient isles; delving into the lore of the regions which inspired her to pen tales of magical realism. Lauren has crossed the Atlantic by boat, passed through Pillars of Hercules and stood aside the ghost of the Colossus of Rhodes which inspired her to pen a fantasy which is a work in progress.

Born and raised in Southern California, she divides her time between the Sierras of Nevada and the Santa Barbara Coast of California. She currently resides in Nevada. And loves dogs.

www.laurennapa.com